Part One:

Summer

ONE

The chimes of the public address system echoed around the park, between the dour wooden buildings, most repurposed military huts from the war. The rain bounced off the paving stones, rustled the long grass, and disturbed the bunting.

"Good morning campers!" A cheerful voice promised, as I hurried through the camp. "The weather has conspired against us, but we will still have a jolly time today. The Tea Dance Four will be in later, to get your hips shaking. They are the valley's own answer to the Four Aces, you know."

If you listened very carefully, you could hear campers trying, and failing, to imagine anything worse.

"But this morning, your young'uns can join Muddles the Clown in the club house, while you hide in the canteen for elevensies. Hows about that my darlings?"

I hurried my step, to beat the children to the clubhouse.

*

The children sat around the floor of the clubhouse giggled and snorted as I failed to find a coin behind the ear of Jessica, my brave volunteer. She was at the older end of my audience, maybe eleven years old, in a light summer top, and a three quarter length skirt, with thick glasses perched on her nose.

I rolled my eyes, and produced a large, boxy, torch from my battered leather surgeon's bag, to shine into her ear, tutting and muttering as I did so. Then brightening my expression with a raised eyebrow. "Ah, there we are! It got stuck!"

My current performance was as Muddles The Clown. My face was painted, my shoulders slouched, and my gait slouched and laconic beneath a big shapeless jacket of a loudly colourful plaid, a wig of ginger curls protruding from under my bowler hat. I had rounded off the sharp edges of my voice, and moved my accent considerably to the north, placing it on the banks of the Mersey.

"It did?" Jessica asked nervously.

"Yeah, it's my fault. I… miscalculated a little, and got the angle wrong." I took the goldfish bowl from my fold out table and held it close to her head. "Tilt over a little? Wonderful. Would you mind pinching your nose and swallowing, so your ears pop?"

Jessica did as she was told, and I let a cascade of stage-coins pour from my sleeve, careful to position myself so it looked like the cascade was from her ear. The landslide of coins clattered and chimed as they half filled the bowl.

"Better?" I asked.

Jessica grinned and nodded.

One of the Camp staff, in his bottle green blazer and light uniform clapped at the trick, encouraging the children to applaud me. Even a few of the adults, hiding from the rain at the bar, over in the back corner of the clubhouse, joined in (although their applause was polite rather than enthusiastic).

I rewarded Jessica with one of the Sunrise Valley

Holiday Camp pin badges I was supposed to give to good sports, and ushered her back amongst the kids.

Outside the British summertime was playing true to form, and heavy rain was pelting down over the swimming pool, sun loungers, and tennis courts. Clouds blotted the sky. Thunder rumbled, and the guttering on the "chalets" (that looked a lot more like sheds, despite the Wendy-house paintwork and window boxes) were overflowing, turning the concrete footpaths around the camp into rivers, and the wide lawns into quagmires.

'Woody' Chuck, the Camp's hefty, jowly, MC was lurking by the bar, with a cigarette and a pint of bitter. He looked up at me, and subtly gestured to his watch, reminding me I had five minutes until we needed to clear the kids club out, so he could prepare for the (recently relocated) knobbly knee contest.

I chose my last two volunteers of the morning (Morris and Emma, twin seven year olds) and invited them to join me on the floor. I produced a deck of cards from my fingertips, in each hand, with a flourish. A red pack in the left, that I gave to Morris, and a blue deck in my right, which I gave to Emma. "Neither of you are professional gamblers or card sharks are you?"

They shook their heads.

"Sorry…" I lowered my voice to a stage whisper. "I have to ask." They didn't find that funny. I can't blame them. I got them to shuffle their decks for a while, then crouched to talk to address Morris. "Now, Morris, do you have a favourite card?"

He looked blank. "I dunno."

"Ah." I held up a finger. "You see, if what a magician normally does is takes the deck from you, fans out a bunch of cards, and then tells you to pick one." I took his deck, and fanned it out to show him. "The trick is, that I secretly, subtly, without your knowing, urge you to take the card I want you to take."

One of the card slithered up from the fan, and wriggled for attention. I poked it back into place, tapped the deck back into shape. I handed it to Morris.

There was movement in the corner of my eye. A few early arrivals for the Knobbly Knees contest were settling in at the bar. One of them, a young woman, with a round, open face, teddy bear build, and enthusiastic grin, lurked at the back of my audience, sipping half a mild, as she watched me. She was dressed for a hike, in a short-sleeved shirt, tank top sweater, and long shorts, over comfortable shoes.

"A much better trick," I said to Morris, "would be for you to choose a card now. Your favourite card… Or any that pops in your head."

"Like the Jack of Hearts?" He asked.

I split the deck, and revealed the Jack of Hearts. "A good choice. Now, take your card, and this pen, and… draw on it. Draw anything you like, so you know this card is yours."

Morris gleefully scrawled glasses, a curly moustache, and a pirate hat on the jack.

I shuffled the defaced Jack back into the deck, with

some fancy moves, springing the card from hand to the other, and fanning two halves of the deck together. As I did it, I looked over at Emma. "You see, Emma, I'm doing all this, because these fancy flourishes trick people into thinking that there is no possible way, I can be carefully counting the cards, and tracking exact location of your brother's card. Look at this." I turned back to Morris, and cut the deck, revealing a pristine Jack of Hearts. "Is this your…" I trailed off and did a double take, my brow pinching. "No. It's the wrong Jack of Hearts." I plucked the card from the deck, and pretended to throw it away, vanishing it with a flick of my fingers. I shuffled the deck again, and split it, to reveal another (or rather, the same) pristine Jack of Hearts. Again I pretended to toss it away, and again, I shuffled the deck, only to find it, once again, when I split the deck.

This time I pretended to notice the blue back of the card.

I clicked my fingers. "Oh… I see what happened…" I walked over to Emme and gave her a big, cheesy, grin.

"Emma. Should I have asked if you were a thief?"

She giggled.

"Do you know where your brother's card is?" I asked.

"In here," she said, offering me the deck.

I nodded.

She smiled.

"Cut the deck for me?" I asked.

Emma cut the deck.

I gave a triumphant cry, and snatched the card away before she, or anybody else could see it, and swapped it for her brother's defaced Jack in the same movement. I held Morris's Jack out for everybody to see. "Boys and girls, if you could please show your appreciation to Emma and Morris!" I gave the two volunteers their badges, and took my bow.

The woman at the back of the audience clapped cheered as loud as the children.

I took my table and bag of props, and marched happily away, leaving the Camp staff to say the final few words, and dismiss the kids, shooing them off to lunch in the canteen.

*

I trudged through the rain to my "villa" (a shed like cabin that was considerably less cheerfully decorated than the chalets) through the rain. It wasn't the worst digs I had taken for a job. There was one main room, with inconveniently space saving furniture, and one corner boxed off into a cramped washroom. Cat-swinging was not an option.

I packed away my props, shrugged off my costume, and set about scouring the makeup from my face.

I spent no time as myself, if such a thing was even possible, and instead immediately began my transformation into Professor Magpie, who would be entertaining happy campers poolside in the afternoon with card tricks and small illusions, and as part of the evening's festivities in the Clubhouse.

Professor Magpie (often billed as the Magical Professor Magpie) was a dapper gent, in a simple tweed suit, dark shirt, and old school tie. I straightened my hair, and put on my prop glasses, and considered myself in the mirror.

"Hello," I said, as Muddles. I rubbed my cheeks and pursed my lips, "Hello," I said, again, this time moving my accent South, and refining it through an expensive education, and a respectable background. "Hello," I said, as the Professor. "And how are you finding your stay with us?"

Satisfied, I put a kettle to boil on the baby electric stove, and went to lurk under my doorway, watching the rain while I waited for it to boil.

My neighbour was doing the same, smoking a cigarette. Doris was a tall, athletic, girl, with a straight back, and squared shoulders, usually dressed for the sports activities, in a polo shirt and a snug pair of shorts under her blazer.

She glanced my way, and smiled. "Hey…" She said with an enthusiasm she had never shown me before. "Hello!"

"Hello!" I said, offering her a smile.

She pointed at me. "You're pretty handy with a deck of cards, aren't you?"

I felt the weight of the inevitable on my shoulders. "Why?"

Her eyes lit up. "Because I think you might be just the man to help me give a turd of a man the boot up the arse he so richly deserves."

I wasn't sure how I should have responded to that, so I hid behind the Professor's genteel calm, and gestured at my door. "Well, I have a kettle on. Would you like a cup of tea, perhaps?"

Doris nodded. "I think I would."

Two

Doris perched on my bed, and sipped her tea from a cup that she held so tight her knuckles bleached. I worried that the delicate china would crack in her hands. Her eyes were bright, and she made a valiant attempt at a smile, but it was unconvincing. Every other muscle in her body was knotted tight and her last nerve was ready to snap.

She let out a long, weary, breath. "His name is Charles. He… holidays along the coast a way. His family have a house there, a… manor, for the summer. Last year we had… we were close. We met in town, on the pier, at the shooting gallery. We were both trying our hand, and we got talking. There was a… lightning bolt, a connection, and when we ended up in the same pub, an hour or two later it seemed like fate. By any reasonable means, we should have never known each other. He was born with a silver spoon in his mouth, dresses like a prince, and has one of those laughs. But…

there is something else there too. He can be kind, and sweet, and poetic. He cares about things, and sometimes, when he's talking about something in the newspaper, something that might as well be alien to us, his eyes go out of focus, and you can see he's thinking about it, seeing the world through their eyes, feeling their pain. Behind the bluff, and the swagger, there was a delicate little poet I wanted to protect. To hold. I thought he only showed that to me. I thought we were in love, I thought… it was something. And when the summer ended, and he promised to look me up, to write, I believed him. I dreamt of the moment I would hear from him, of meeting him on the town, of us being… us again."

She trailed off, and watched the rain on the window.

"It didn't happen?" I asked.

She snorted. "No. The dream faded, and didn't die. Instead I sat around, wondering if maybe when I was back here, we would cross paths, and he would explain how he lost my address, or something had happened, or we would just share a look and not need words. Hope is cruel like that.

It's barbed and needs to be ripped away painfully."

I offered her one of my handkerchiefs (careful not to pass her a trick one). "And it was ripped from you?"

Doris nodded. "Can I tell you a secret?"

"Anything you tell me will be held in confidence," I promised her. "Magicians put a lot of stock in the value of a secret."

"A few of us, from the camp, sometimes, when we have a free evening, and need a little extra cash, we can earn a little in town. There's a nightclub in Chapel Bay. It's always fairly clean, and smartly run. In the summer season it can be busy, and they tend to need extra help. You can make good money, but the night is long, you never get a spare moment, and tottering around in heels can be murder on the feet. I've seen it from both sides. Charles used to like to go there on dates. He could always find a card game there, always poker, and… Charles always wins."

That intrigued me. "Always?"

She smiled. "He said that in London he earned more in

the casinos than he did in the city. He said he had a system."

She closed her eyes. "Anyway, this summer, like any other, I took a few cash in hand shifts to help at the club, and… one night there he was, in one of the side rooms, playing cards, making his money. Our eyes met. The lightning bolt didn't happen. His smile didn't happen. Instead his eyes were cold, and hard, and his lips pressed thin into a flat smile. Still my heart started pounding, and I felt weightless on my feet again. I made sure he saw my smile, before I walked away, and a little later, when I was having a cigarette by the back door, he walked out to join me. I really thought, I really hoped…" She broke into a sob, and sipped on her tea, as she steeled herself before she continued. "He stood over me, and he kind of cornered me. His eyes were like a shark. I said… something. That I missed him, I think, and I was so happy to see him again, but… he told me I wasn't going to see him again. There wasn't an us. There hadn't been since he slipped out the bed that last morning. The promise to write, the kiss goodbye, it was all part of the game, and I was… spoiled fruit now. There was no sport in me." She looked at her hands. "And that's all I was. Sport. Everything I thought we had, all those memories dearest to my heart were… broken. I was…"

I offered her a handkerchief to wipe away her tears. "I'm sorry. I can only imagine."

Doris straightened herself, and adjusted her blazer. "He walked away, and spoke to one of the waiters, Billy, his favourite, and said he should keep an eye on me, to make sure I hold my tongue." She leant forward. "Anyway, I asked Charles about his system once. He told me it was the stuff you do. He watches a fresh deck being shuffled, and follows the cards, mapping them in his mind, knowing his opponent's cards. He said he would fold early on some hands, because you have to lose a few hands to win the game. He said if you unwrap a pack of cards, and shuffled it, he could tell you the order of the cards without seeing their faces." She stared at me. "Can you do that?"

I gave her a sorrowful smile. "I'm sorry, but, no, I

can't, and neither can her. That is what I claim to do, what I make the illusion of doing, because it is just a trick. I make it look like I can do the impossible, and I dress it up in a nice story as part of the misdirection. There are systems people have, but they are about calculating the odds that another hand is better or worse than yours. In blackjack, you can never know what cards the dealer will give you next, but you can try and calculate the odds of it favouring your hand over his."

Doris nodded. "Yeah. I thought so. You see… what he said to Billy sat wrong with me. Why would he care what I said? If I'm sport, then I'm… a notch on his bedpost. One of his trophies. But… I had asked about his system. And if he lied to me about it… then maybe there's something he's hiding. Maybe he just cheats. And…"

"Maybe his friends wouldn't want to work that out?" I asked.

Doris nodded. "Maybe I can humble him a little."

"With a little help?" I offered.

Doris smiled. "I would appreciate that."

*

The rain did not relent in the afternoon, so instead of performing at the poolside, I made my way around the bar at the clubhouse, offering some mild distractions to some of the campers, while the afternoon tea dance was prepared. They were simple effects, a few with cards, some with coins, and the occasional escape from handcuffs.

Slowly the crowd began to grow, with more jackets and ties, swing dresses and smart skirts, as the campers donned their Sunday best, for the tea dance.

Soon enough the band took to the stage, and Woody Chuck stepped up to the microphone. The crowd drifted from the bar to the dancefloor, as music filled the clubhouse. The girl dressed for a hike remained at the bar. She watched the dance, her eyes wide, and a big smile on her lips.

I approached her cautiously. "Ma'am?"

She flashed me a grin. "Oh, hello. Sorry." She waved a hand at herself. "I... had a little accident with my packing, and don't have a dress."

"I am sure nobody minds," I said. "Would you care to join in? Or to mingle?"

She chuckled. "I would mind. I just came second in a knobbly knees contest. I always thought my knees were fine, but I never thought they were knobbly!" She glanced around. "Besides, sooner or later somebody interesting will want a drink, and… stood here, away from the band, we can hear each other talk. So… are you interesting Professor?"

"I try to be," I admitted.

She smiled, and offered me her hand. "Harry."

"Simon." I said, in my own accent, shaking her hand.

THREE

We sat in a quiet corner.

Harry watched me over her pint glass, as she drank her mild, and toyed with her hair. "So," she said, with a curious smile. "Where are you really from Muddles?"

"London," I admitted. "More or less. It's… a little complicated."

Harry laughed. "Oh, I know the feeling."

"And you?"

"London," she said, with a smile. "More or less." She pointed a finger at me. "It's boring. I don't want to think about it, let alone talk about it. I'm here to escape. So…" She looked at me. "You were Muddles the clown too, weren't you?"

I nodded.

"Can I ask how you did the trick with the cards?" She asked.

"If you did, I would have to tell you it was a secret."

"Ah." She tapped her lips. "How about if asked how you came to be here?"

"I have an agent," I said, with a thin smile. "They offered me the booking, and I took it. It's a season long engagement, that doesn't pay too badly when you consider I get room and board, as homely as they are, and it's an awful lot better than being hungry and evicted."

She raised an eyebrow. "Does that happen?"

"It's a danger." I gave her a smile. "I've worked just hard enough to make life difficult for myself. I have built a good reputation, which meant that a few years back, I had to give up the day job and stop taking little side gigs for pin money, and make a career of this. I'm good, and reliable, but I'm not a Headliner. Every summer I've always found an engagement, somewhere like this, on a pier, or at an amusement park, and every winter I've managed to find work in pantomimes. The rest of the year can be pretty lean. It's hit or miss if I can get a supporting gig to fill a slot in a cabaret, or on a touring variety show. Times can get very lean, and I usually have to fall back onto other work. Luckily I have a few friends who are always grateful for an extra pair of hands hauling sack barrows around Covent Garden.”

Harry pursed her lips. “It sounds like an adventure, and it’ll be worth it one day, when your name is in lights, somewhere.”

“There are a lot of us who never become a Headliner,” I warned her.

She nodded. “And there are a lot of us who never amount to anything much at all.”

“What do you do, Harry?” I asked.

“I’m…” She looked away, as though embarrassed. “I work for Rochelle’s, the department store.”

“Oh?” I smiled. “Which floor?”

“Eleventh,” she said. “Up in the offices.”

“So…” I cocked my head. “A secretary? Or in the phone pool?”

She shook her head. “Oh, something far more boring

than that. I'm… nothing. I'm the least important cog in the machine. I could run off to join the circus and I honestly don't think anybody would notice." There was a genuine sadness in her voice. "I'm not important."

"I promise you," I said, gently, "that you are."

She stared at me. "You wouldn't know. You know nothing about me."

"I know you don't like to dance, but do like clowns," I said. "And I know you are kind, because you bothered to talk to me." I held up a finger. "Most importantly of all, I know you are wrong. That's the thing about cogs, machines need all of them. They are all important. It's just some are better paid. Rochelle and Sons is a wonderful shop, but how long it will remain the envy of the world without shelves being stacked, or the floors being cleaned? How can the buyers work without secretaries or the telephone pool? How can the warehouse work without clerks processing the orders?" I smiled at her. "And I know you have family. Nobody comes here alone. Somebody loves you enough to worry about you."

Harry smiled. "Maybe you are right. Maybe…" She cupped my cheek. "You have been too kind to me. I think, maybe, you really should be a professor."

"Well, I do perform Punch and Judy shows, so, technically…" I smiled at her, and checked my watch. "I have to go and prepare for the evening show."

"Ah." She looked at her hands. "I'm sorry. I have… other plans for the evening."

"It's a small park, and the coach doesn't return to London for a few days, so, perhaps we will bump into each other again." I paused a moment. "If you would like?"

Harry paused, her eyes suddenly heavy. "Oh, I would, but… I don't think… I'm sorry. I…"

"Oh." I held up my hands. "I'm sorry. I did not mean that to sound like it was an invitation to anything untoward. I just…"

"I really would like that," Harry said, rising to her feet, "but it won't happen. Sorry. I have to go." She stepped away.

"Sorry."

In a few moments she had vanished out of the clubhouse, swallowed whole by the storm.

*

Harry was nowhere to be seen over the next few days.

I kept an eye out for her, amongst the crowds in the group events. I saw huddles of other women and girls from the London coach, but she was never with them. I lurked at the fringe of the crowd for the Miss Sunrise pageant, and the party games, but our paths simply didn't cross.

Then Friday morning rolled around, and the London coaches rumbled away. The little thread of hope that there might ever have been anything more from our conversation, the little spark of desire, faded away. Life went on, and I carried on with my duties, hiding my pangs of disappointment behind my plastic smile.

That morning, my duties largely involved helping Doris decorate the clubhouse with balloons and bunting, to welcome the fresh coaches that afternoon.

"Cheer up!" Doris said, pinging a balloon at my head. "It might never happen."

"Well, that's the problem," I said.

She looked at me, an eyebrow raised. "Oh, aye?"

I shrugged. "Somebody seemed interested, and for a while I thought it might, but… then I said something and I'm pretty sure that she spent the rest of her stay avoiding me."

Doris giggled. "Oh, I see. You bowled yourself a googly?"

"I think so."

"Happens to the best of us." She grinned. "And it is definitely her loss."

"It was nothing." I chewed my lip. "I was… I thought too much of a very small moment."

"Ah." Doris gave me a sage look. "But small moments can be some of the most important. Small moments can be nice. I like the small moments."

I dropped the last few balloons into the net, and carefully hoisted it up to the ceiling, ready to be released on cue. "Well, I don't really get many small moments. Nobody ever finds me interesting enough to spare me a small moment."

Doris chuckled. "You don't have to be interesting. You're..."

"I'm what?" I asked.

She giggled. "Not everybody wants to be swept away by a whirlwind. Some people appreciate the... other kinds of nice."

"The less exciting kinds?" I asked.

She put her hands on my chest. "Look, if you help me with my Charles problem tomorrow, then I will find you somebody to have a slightly more promising little moment with. How about that?"

"You don't have to," I said.

She grinned. "I like a challenge."

"But..." I cleared my throat. "I'm helping a friend. You don't owe me a favour."

Something softened behind her eyes. "Well... maybe I

want to show I appreciate it. Don't worry. We'll think of something."

There was mischief in her smile.

FOUR

I dressed as the Professor to go to the nightclub. His suits were my smartest clothes. We rode into town on Doris's little motorcycle. She wore a an old aviator's jacket over her midnight blue sheath dress, and had me hold her dangerous heels, while she rode in steel capped boots.

The machine roared around the country lanes, howling like a banshee when she opened the throttle on the straight roads. I'm not sure how fast we were going. I got too scared when we overtook the sports car, and had to close my eyes and grip her waist for dear life.

We flew down the seafront well above the speed limit, and squalled to a halt at the promenade.

"You can let go now," Doris said, curtly.

"Sorry." I felt my cheeks burn. "Those bends were rather… and you banked… and…"

She laughed, and nodded at her feet. "A little help?"

I hopped off the bike and unlaced one of her boots for her.

"Make one joke about the smell," she said, with a sharp undertone to her voice, "and I will kick you."

"I wouldn't dare," I said.

"Good," she slipped her foot into the shoe.

I unlaced the other boot. "I'll just buy you a little hamper of scented soaps for Christmas."

"Ha. Funny." She shoved her stockinged toes in my face, and shoved me playfully away. "You daft git. You best not make that kind of joke in the club."

"What kind should I make?" I asked.

She rolled her eyes. "Maybe you should play the strong silent type." She hopped off the bike and took my arm. "Well… the silent type."

We hurried up the steps to the nightclub, and checked our helmets, overcoats, and boots at the cloak room. The attendant gave Doris a familiar smile, and made a little small talk, about jokes I didn't understand. The Brigadier had been up to his old tricks, and Chancer was on good form.

"Is there a game on?" Doris asked. "The Professor here is a bit of a player when it comes to cards."

"Is he?" The attendant gave me an appraising look. "He should have a word with Billy then."

Doris took my arm, and escorted me through the club. The dance floor was busy, and a band was rocking and rolling on the stage. We passed the bar and walked up the stairs, to where a scrawny, oily, looking waiter, with slicked back hair, and a sloping brow, stood guard by a set of double doors.

"What do you want?" He asked.

I stepped forwards, before Doris could speak. "Sorry, she didn't want to come, but there was a game on, and I insisted she at least tried to get me through the door."

Doris said. "His money's good."

Billy stepped forward. "And who do you know with money?"

"A friend," I repeated, plucking a roll of notes from my

pocket, and peeling a few off. "A generous one."

He snatched the offered bribe, and studied the note. "I guess your money is as good as anybody else's."

We walked past him into the room.

There was one table. It was oak, old and solid, made back when furniture was built to last for generations, and polished as smooth as glass. A few men in suits, or smart blazers, sat about the table, watched by a handful of men and women, lurking around the edge of the room. A fog of smoke hung over the table, coiling and billowing.

Charles was easy to spot. He and Doris shared a long, hard, gaze of the kind that stopped time, for a few heartbeats. It made her squeeze my arm until her knuckles bleached, and her jaw to set firm.

He was sat at what would have been the head of the table, when it was used for business, under the austere gaze of a noble old oil painting of a Georgian soldier, carrying himself like he was holding court. He was rangy, with a beak of a nose, wearing a scarlet velvet jacket over an embroidered waistcoat that suggested something of the Byronic.

Next, clockwise around the table, was a conservatively dressed older man, with a bald head, bushy moustache, and a pin striped suit of the timeless cut favoured by solicitors and bank managers. His tie and clip both bore a regimental crest. He was shuffling a deck of cards, and wore the green visor that marked him as tonight's dealer.

The other player was a dapper young man, with a neatly trimmed beard, and a rubbery, expressive, face in a tan sports jacket, over a sand coloured suit, in a fashionable cut. He gave me a cheerful nod, and gestured to the empty seat. "Ah. This makes things interesting."

Harry was stood behind him, in a dress that nipped and tucked to flatter her build, and a matching jacket, decorated by a rose shaped broach, of red ceramics, set in bright gold. Her smile wavered, then brightened when she saw me.

"Does anybody mind?" I asked.

"Not at all." The bank manager said, waving for me to

sit. "Not at all."

The Dapper Chap looked at my tie, then at me. Sitting closer I could see his beard covered some scars beneath one corner of his mouth, and across his chin. He offered me his hand. "Danny. This is Puck and Charles. You don't have to call Puck Reverend. He's off the clock."

The dealer chuckled, a deep rumbling laugh, tarnished by years of whiskey and cigars. "And anything that happens behind closed doors is under confessional rules."

"Simon," I said.

Charles smirked, glancing up at Doris. "And where did you find him?"

Doris did not hesitate. "The retreat in Hythe. The Professor was sent there by his doctor, under strict orders to have less work, and more exercise. I gave him tennis lessons."

"Professor of what?" Puck asked, dealing the first hand. The conversation continued as we played, through the first round of bets, and into the draw.

I glanced up. Harry looked away, and put a finger to her lips, over a smile. Deep down, I told myself I wasn't lying, I was method acting. "Egyptology," I said, without taking my eyes off her.

Doris raised an eyebrow.

"Egyptology?" Charles asked, draining his glass. "And where did you study that?"

"London. We took a school trip to see the collection in the college museum when I was fourteen, and I decided there and then. My history master had something of a love of the subject, and instilled it in as many of us as he could."

"At Willow Lake?" Charles asked, pointing at my tie.

"Yes." I looked straight into his eye, and smiled. "My old history teacher was a little obsessed. His room in the dormitory was decorated with all kinds of Egyptian knick-knacks, and his office had a mummified crocodile suspended from the ceiling. You know, when I think back, I can still smell it."

Puck laughed, and nodded. "I can only imagine."

Charles began the next round of bets, peeling a conservative little stake from his billfold, and dropping it on the table. He tapped his ear with a nervous finger, an action that became a habit of his through the night. "Oh, my round, by the way. I'll have a vodka martini, Reverend?"

"Brandy," Puck said, glowering at his hand.

"Whiskey," Danny said.

"Whiskey and ginger wine," I said, placing my bet.

The game progressed, like a pressure cooker reaching the boil.

Billy strolled around the table, delivering drinks. He swept out of the room, and the final round of bets were placed. Charlie folded early, Danny took the hand, with an impressive three sevens.

There was little chat on the second round. The pleasantries were passed, and the game became serious. Charles bet big to begin with, trying to drive up the stakes, until we had our round of coffees. Then he folded. As the Reverend scooped up the deck to shuffle, he knocked the spent cards the wrong way, and I noticed that Charles folded on a strong hand, which only made sense if he knew I had a flush.

I saw his method, but played the next two rounds, to be sure. In both of them Charles came back strong, gouging deep into Danny's bank.

In the third round both Danny and Charles were making confident bets, raising the stakes and applying the pressure. Charles was stony faced, hiding his tells well, but that finger tapped at his ear.

Billy glanced through the door. "Drinks sirs?"

"Coffees," Danny said. "If we are all agreed."

"On my tab, of course," I said. "It must be my turn."

We had another round of bets, before the coffees were delivered. As Billy stepped over to deliver my coffee, I leapt to my feet, and shoved him against the wall. The coffee crashed to the floor.

Charles and Danny leapt to their feet.

Puck's jaw dropped. "What is this?"

I reached under Billy's dinner jacket, and found his little transmitter. It was an expensive, compact model. "This?" I said. "This is a man paid to look at our cards as he delivers our drinks, looking in the silver tray if he can't see them directly. Then he whispers them into this, so somebody knows if their bets are safe or not."

I pressed the transmit button, and held it out close to Danny, then Puck, then at Charles. Feedback wailed, and Charles winced in pain, snatching an earpiece from under his long hair. "Unless, of course, you have an explanation for this?"

Charles stared at Doris. "She did this! She did this!"

Doris folded her arms. "You think I brought a friend here to get conned? I just wanted to see the smirk wiped from your face when you lost."

"So?" Charles stood, straightened his jacket, and stared daggers at Doris. He reached over to take his money back out the pot. "I lose a game. I lose money. You are still nothing, and I will always be¬"

"A git," Danny said, grabbing Charles' wrist, and twisting it, until he dropped the fistful of notes back into the pot. "That stays where it is, old chap. You get to bugger off."

Puck nodded. "Don't expect to be welcome back."

Charles shook his head. "Now listen here…"

"Yes!" Puck groaned, bored. "We know who you are. Daddy will have his say. You will still be told to bugger off. Goodbye."

Charles stormed away.

Puck looked at me. "Well? Are you betting or folding?"

I placed my bet.

FIVE

Harry laughed so hard she almost choked on her cocktail. "But, why did you sit there as the Professor? Why the subterfuge?"

Harry, Danny, Puck, Doris and I were sat around a table in the far corner of the nightclub floor, for our nightcap. Harry was curled against Danny, who had a protective arm over her shoulders. The band were playing the last slow dance of the evening. The game had gone well without Charles. A few hands went back and forth, before luck started favouring my hand. I made a reasonable profit before Danny decided to sensibly cut his losses.

Doris grinned. "That was my idea. We had to be sure that Charley was cheating. If he knew who Simon was, he would know his trick was at risk, and wouldn't give us the chance to expose him."

Puck chuckled. "And of course, nobody here would

know him, except your friends from work, whose sympathies inclined away from Charlie of late."

Doris smiled. "Or so we thought."

Puck cocked his head. "You had me fooled. The talk about Willow Lake Academy, and the details. I can't begin to imagine how you knew all that."

I cleared my throat. "I'm sorry, but that is a trade secret."

Doris cocked her head. "Is it true?"

Puck grinned. "Oh yes. Professor Lintwood's collection is one of the few distinguishing features about Willow Lakes. Once seen, or smelt, it is not easily forgotten."

That was certainly true.

Danny sipped his brandy. "Perhaps, Harry dearest, you could explain how you happen to know that Simon is in fact Muddles the Clown?"

Harry winced, her cheeks burning with colour. "Because I was bored, and it was raining, and… the girls from the telephone pool always make their summers sound like a lark, so… when I took my walk for the day, I happened to walk into the camp, and look around, and…"

"And?" Doris asked, teasingly.

"And apparently my knees are knobbly," Harry said, with a giggle. "It was fun. Although, I suppose I was trespassing, so perhaps I should give my ribbon back!"

I shook my head. "Your secret is safe. Keep it with our blessing."

Doris perked up. She squeaked in sudden delight. "It was you!"

Harry looked confused. "I'm sorry? What was me?"

"The shop girl from Rochelle's!" Doris said. "The one who chatted to Simon, then vanished!"

"Oh!" Harry looked at me. "I suppose I was."

"See!" Doris giggled. "She, you didn't make a girl hide from you until her coach left. You just made her run away never intending to return!"

Danny cocked her head. "Oh, that sounds so much better."

Harry chewed her lip. "I did like our little chat. And…

I didn't lie. I just… might not have told the whole truth, as it

were."

Danny laughed merrily. "My sister the shop girl? Oh,

that is perfect!"

Puck took pity on my confused look and gestured at his

friends. "Might I have the pleasure of introducing you to

Lieutenant Daniel, and Miss Harriet Roschelle."

Doris opened her mouth to say something, but failed.

Her jaw hung slack as she tried again, and again.

Harry let out a sigh, that deflated her. "And this is why

I thought it was easier to…not mention it."

"Rochelle?" Doris managed to splutter. "As in

Rochelle's The Department Store?"

Danny nodded. "Yes."

"And…" Doris gasped. "The Rochelle Fortune?"

Danny gave her a bright smile. "According to the

newspapers."

Harry shrugged a little, and put a fresh cigarette in her

holder. "Believe me, it is a lot less impressive than it sounds."

Doris raised an eyebrow. "Are you sure? I'm pretty impressed."

The last song ran down.

Harry cocked her head. "I suppose, this time we at least get a real goodbye."

"It will be goodbye?" I asked.

Harry smiled. "Why?"

I produced one of my calling cards, with a flourish, from my fingertips. "Well… I did like talking to you, and… if you ever wanted a clown, or a Punch and Judy man, or… to take the offer of a dance…"

Harry hesitantly took the card, and turned it in her fingers. "Or a friend?"

I flushed. "I hoped that went without saying."

She smiled, and tucked the card away. "Good. I like friends. I will write. Promise on my honour." She finished her drink and looked at Danny. "We should be going."

She and Danny linked arms, and walked out of my life.

*

We pulled over to the side of the road long before the gates to the camp, and Doris killed the engine. She glanced over her shoulder at me, and I let go of her hips.

She was smiling under her helmet. "Do you really think she will write to you?"

I shrugged. "It depends if she wants a friend."

"Oh, a friend," Doris said, "or a *friend*."

My cheeks burned. "A friend. Why? Do you think…"

Doris shoved me. "She ran away, and hid. As hints go, that's about as subtle as a sledgehammer to the happy sacks, isn't it?"

We hopped off the bike, and pushed it down the gravel lane to the Camp, on tiptoes as not to disturb anybody.

Doris glanced at me, then pouted. "She's nice, but I don't think her knees are the only thing that's knobbly about her."

"What don't like her?" I asked.

"I like her!" Doris caught her tone, and fought to keep it a whisper. "I just don't think she is who you want your little moments with."

"But…" I counted on my fingers. "She is nice?"

"Yes."

"And she has this smile…"

"I saw that." Doris laughed. "She has a smile for when she thought you were looking."

"And…" I chewed my lip. "She liked talking to me."

"Yeah?" Doris shrugged. "But apparently not enough to care that you were worried for her, or that you thought she was ignoring you. She didn't say sorry."

I looked at my feet. "Oh. I'm sure she didn't mean…"

"No," Doris said, kindly, "she didn't mean a thing. But she didn't say sorry either, and I think maybe my friend deserves a little better." She hesitated a moment. "Like… I appreciate I asked a lot of you tonight, and a lot of it was stuff you weren't comfortable with." She looked at me. "I should probably say thank you."

I grinned. "It's been fun. It was a good night."

There was movement ahead. We ducked into cover against the corner of the pool changing rooms, and watched as Woody Chuck hopped out of somebody else's cabin, in his socks, garters, underpants and string vest. He ran swiftly in the direction of his own accommodation.

"See!" Doris cupped my cheek. "If he can find somebody to share the little moments with, there's hope for you too. When she doesn't write, when she has forgotten she had somebody who thought she was the bees knees, with no idea of her name, or her fortune…remember that even Woody Chuck can find a little moment, so there has to be hope for you."

The coast was clear. We moved on.

At our cabins she chained up the bike and took off her helmet.

I kissed her cheek. "You know that speech isn't going to be worth much if you don't write."

Doris groaned, and rolled her eyes. "I know. I ask a

few little favours, and it causes no end of trouble." She smiled. "You better be worth it."

"I'll try to be," I said, as she reached her front door. "I promise."

She laughed and shook her head.

Part Two:

Winter

Six

Big Al sat in the van, while I loaded the day's deliveries. He was barrel chested and burly, in drab clothes, a donkey jacket, and a flat cap pulled down over his unruly tangle of thinning hair. He had beady eyes, and a moustache you could use to scour dishpans.

I hefted another crate from the sack barrow into the van.

Al poked his head out the van. "Aren't you done yet, Lad? We have a schedule to keep you know. We can't tarry around."

"Oh?" I paused for breath. "Do you think that's why there's meant to be two us doing this? Maybe you could help?"

"I am helping," he said. "I'm doing the thinking. It's the hardest part of the job."

"Want a hand with it?" I asked.

"Just get it done!" Al snorted. He made a point of flicking his newspaper to the racing fixtures, and frowned in concentration as he marked his choices with the stub of a pencil.

I hefted the crates into the van, ferrying them from the warehouse in batches, stacked on the sack barrow.

The morning was dark, and bitterly cold. The spectral fog that blanketed the city was a thick, dirty brown soup of frost and smoke, that blotted out the buildings and painted the world in broad strokes of shadow. It burned my lungs, and made every effort feel heavier.

Eventually I hefted the last crate into place, and strapped our load down.

Al smirked into his newspaper, as I climbed aboard.

"Don't say it," I muttered.

He glanced over at me. "It took you long enough."

I put my head against the cold glass, and watched the world sinking into the abyss of fog, as we drove past. I slipped a shilling and a sixpence from my pocket, and absently practised a series of effects, making them vanish and appear to hop between my hands. Each effect was simple enough, but it was the sequence that strung them together which was important.

I had an audition in a few days, my fourth in a few weeks. It was for a season long engagement, in a pantomime, as one of the pirate crew, who had some funny business with the principal villain, over cursed gold misbehaving.

Al liked to sing while he drove. He only knew a few songs, but he wasn't too sure of the lyrics, and was somewhat uncertain of the melodies. They generally became one song, over the course of a drive, blurring together, with patches of humming to fill in the gaps.

Al remained firmly rooted in the van, for most of our stops. He kept his seat warm, while I delivered orders to pubs, and restaurants about the city. His brief respite from the agonies of 'doing the thinking' was to pull over at a bookmaker's, to ensure his bets were in place before the afternoon's races. On returning to the van, his busy schedule of supervising me resumed, until our last port of call.

From the front, Rochelle's was a building of palatial grandeur, clad in dark stone, haunted by gargoyles, and given colour by stained glass decorations around the edges of the windows. Around the back, however, in the court yard that held the warehouses and loading bays, it was hewn from ancient red brick, with wrought iron fire escapes and drainpipes.

There were two deliveries to make at the store. One was to the staff canteen (in the basement, with a reasonable chance of being offered a cup of tea and some biscuits), and one to the restaurant, on the ninth floor (with no prospect of refreshments).

I held up a coin to Al. "I don't suppose you want to flip for it?"

He shook his head. "Try and be a bit quicker about this one, eh lad. We don't want to be getting back to the yard late, do we?"

I loaded a barrow with the crates for the restaurant

kitchen, and trundled off through the loading docks to the antique cargo lift. Bert, the operator, was a friendly old man, with a lopsided smile, who had been with the store for longer than anybody could remember. There were rumours he had been with the store since it opened. There were those who (only half) joked that he may actually be a ghost, haunting the store.

"Afternoon, Bert," I said.

He slid the cage door closed, and looked me up and down. "Ninth floor is it?"

"If you please," I said.

He raised an eyebrow at me, expectantly.

I took a bag of plums from my coat pocket, and tossed them to him. He caught them with the ease of a seasoned cricketer, and checked the contents. They vanished under his long coat, before anybody could spot them. He cranked the handle, and there was a smell of bumper cars, as the cage rattled its way slowly up the shaft.

"Any good gossip?" I asked.

Bert shook his head. "Nah mate. There's all kinds of stuff going on up on the Eleventh, but it's all board members, and shareholders, and the like. Doesn't matter a gnat's fart to me. They'll still need shelves stacked and this handle yanked."

A memory of Harry's smile fleetingly sparked at the back of my mind. I buried it deep, before it stirred up all those awkward little questions: if she ever thought of me, and if she ever considered writing, if those little moments had meant anything to her as they had to me?

The promise to write, had never been filled.

Doris, on the other hand, wrote once a week, without fail, even if it was only to complain that she had nothing of interest to write about. I wrote back in the evening, and posted my reply on my way to work the next morning. Her letters had been coming a lot more often since she had been swept off her feet by a young man whom I could only imagine to be dashingly handsome and something of a poet. She had fallen for him in a matter of weeks, and they had been living together for a few months now.

Doris had made taken exceptional glee in describing how her landlady believed they were married (and how she would not have been able to rent the flat if the truth was known), how exciting it was to be living the lie, and how much she wished it to be true.

Sometimes her letters mentioned other friends, and I often wondered how many of her secrets she confided with them. Or why she confided in me.

I had more or less convinced myself it was because I knew precisely none of the others mentioned in her letters. I was safely distant from her life.

The carriage slowed into the ninth floor, and Bert pulled the cage open for me.

I followed the drab service corridor around the back of the building. The white washed walls and concrete floor was a world away from the regal opulence of the restaurant. My footsteps echoed around me.

As I rounded the corner, I came to a sudden, grinding,

halt. A chef, and two workmen were blocking the corridor with a step ladder.

"Leave them there!" The chef directed me. "Looks like we are going to have to clear out the kitchen, anyway."

I looked at them. "What's up?"

"A biblical plague," one of the workmen said. "Insects in the kitchen, probably a dead rat or something. We'll find it."

The chef took my clipboard, and signed for the delivery.

One of the workmen hopped up the ladder, and lifted down a hatch in the ceiling, exposing a loom of pipes and cables, all wrapped in asbestos bandaging. Dead flies poured out over the floor. Live flies buzzed and swarmed around him.

The chef threw his hands up in despair. "Fan-bloody-tastic!"

"See!" The workman said, choking on insects. "Biblical!"

I slid the stack off my barrow, and made good my escape.

*

The bus rumbled through the city.

I was still practising my sequence for the audition, with the sixpence and shilling. My fellow commuters were making a point of not looking at me, perhaps worried I would try and impress them. I was concentrating on the sequence so completely I almost rode the bus all the way home out of habit. The bus had already stopped by the time I realised we were at the stop by the newsagent, and I had to grab my satchel and run to make it off, against the tide of new passengers. I hopped out the back of the bus into the street, and walked briskly under the railway, to the lockups.

In the corner of my eye, I glimpsed somebody else making a last moment dash off the bus, hopping off as it pulled away. I got a glimpse of somebody in a dark blue, naval style overcoat, and black fedora. A big man, a giant, taller than me, and as broad across the shoulders as he stood tall.

The giant stepped into the crowd, and was lost from my view.

My lockup was a Victorian railway arch, closed off by heavy wooden doors. I dug my keys from my satchel, and let myself in. Running down one side of the arch was a worktop, fitted with my tools and vices. On the other were the shelving units in which my props and gadgets were neatly wrapped and stacked.

My latest project was on the workbench, in pieces. A work in progress. The air still smelt of the black silk paint I had sprayed the outer casing in, and the glue I had used, a heady cocktail of fumes that hadn't quite faded. I set my satchel on the side, and took out the box of springs that had finally arrived in that morning's post.

I spent two hours (and change) assembling the device, learning the knack for fitting the springs, and ensuring all the moving parts ran free. Before mounting the device on a leather strap, and putting it anywhere near my wrist, I put it in the vice. I loaded each of the three chambers with a penny, and primed them a winding key, until the mechanism clicked and set.

"Ladies and gentlemen," I said, in the Professor's voice, "whatever they might tell you, a good magician always has something up their sleeve."

I tapped the plate under the device.

The first penny launched, with a low thud of releasing springs. It was supposed to fly up, maybe a foot, or two, and drop neatly into my waiting hand.

It did not.

Instead it shot straight up, so fast that it half buried itself in the bricks of the ceiling.

"Ah," I whispered. "I may have miscalculated."

I fired the other two coins, and they too punched themselves into the ceiling.

I rubbed my eyes, and considered the alterations required to the set up. It had been a long day, and I was too tried to strip it down and figure out the adjustments. I made it safe, and locked it in my strong box, with the flash paper and other dangerous materials. I put the drawings in the safe, with the rest of my drawings and documents (not to mention the biscuit tin with the mementos of my Service).

My stomach growled, strongly suggesting a visit to the chip shop, on my way home. I stepped out the lock up, and snapped the padlock on the doors.

Old instincts twitched. Hairs prickled the back of my neck. There was somebody watching me from the shadows.

I turned, bringing up my elbow to defend myself as somebody burst from the shadows. I blocked them from grappling me, but they were too fast, and too close for me to fight back. In the fraction of a second before the fist hit me like a battering ram, I had a fleeting impression of a naval style coat, and a fedora. A shape that was big, and broad, a hulking bear of a man.

The guy from the bus.

The punch snapped my head back, and my brain bounced off my skull. My vision blurred, the world wobbled, and my knees gave way. Another punch landed, and almost tore my head off. The world went dark and dull for a few moments. When I blinked it back to sharp focus, I was pinned to the door of my lockup by a gloved hand crushing my throat.

Somebody was shouting at me in a harsh Glasgow accent, but I couldn't make out their words.

I drover my knee into their groin. They didn't flinch. I clawed at their hand, but couldn't budge it.

"Where," the figure asked, angrily, "is he?"

"Huh?" I slurred. "Who?"

"Rochelle. Danny Rochelle!" The man in the fedora snapped. He was past sixty, and was all eyebrows and cheekbones, with skin like parchment. "Where is he?"

I blinked. "I don't know. Why would I know?"

The Scotsman glared at me with poisonous eyes. "Don't play games. Where is he?"

I gave him a helpless look.

"Fine," the Scotsman said, at last. "Well, when you see

him, tell him Conrad Drake wants a word, eh?"

His head swung back, and he lunged forwards. His head cracked against mine, so hard that a wet, red, pain crunched inside skull. My body went limp, and the cobbles swooped up catch me. His boot slammed down onto my ribs, in a stamping, stomping, kick, over and again.

Seven

Detective Inspector Plummer sighed and rubbed his jowls. He was sat beside my hospital bed, with a notepad, and pen. He was a leathery figure, forged and tempered by a life of hard knocks, with something of the stoat about his features. "The thug thought you were Daniel Rochelle, as in…the shop with the hampers?"

"No." I held up a finger. "He thought Danny had been in touch with me."

"Ah." He crossed out a note, and made another. "And do you… know Rochelle?"

My body was camouflaged with bruises, mottled in shades of purple and blue. My lip was spit, and my nose broken. I had three cracked ribs, and two missing teeth. Every breath hurt me all over.

The other patients in the ward were doing their best not to be interested, to stare at their newspapers, or find sudden fascination in the view out the tall, gallery windows. Nurses stood at their station, stealing glances in our direction.

I took my time, before speaking. "I met him and his sister once. We played cards. We chatted a while."

Plummer cocked his head. "But, he thought you were… more? Why?"

"I don't know," I said, quietly.

"And he said something about Conrad Drake. Who is that?"

I shook my head. "I have no idea."

"What did you do in your service?" Plummer asked, in a tone that suggested he already knew.

"I was with the Royal Artillery."

He nodded. "You saw action?"

Again, there was something that suggested he already knew.

"Unfortunately. Yes." I looked at him. "Is that important?"

"You were with the Royal Artillery, but Malaya was

not an artillery war, you were doing old fashioned soldiering, weren't you? And you won a commendation."

"It was a police action. I took a few prisoners." I rubbed the back of my neck. "I talked better than I fought."

"Nevertheless, you are not unskilled, and this man bested you."

"True." I rubbed the back of my neck. "If he'd been half a mile away, and I had a twenty five pounder cannon, things would have been very different. But it turns out, my attacker wasn't fighting an artillery war either. It just feels like he was."

There was something in Plummer's eyes, that suggested the transistors firing and relays clattering behind, as he fed my statement through the machinery of logic. "This attack was too well planned be over... nothing. Are you sure the name means nothing to you?"

I winced. "Never heard of it."

"No." Plummer tapped his pen to his lip. "Very... curious." He snapped his notebook closed, and rose to his feet. "Rest assured, we will do all we can to find the man who did this."

"And…" I sat up, which felt like being hit by a runaway steam roller. "You will tell Harry and Danny, the Rochelles? If he wants to hurt them... You will warn them? Please?"

Plummer nodded, with a little hesitation. "The matter is well in hand, son."

When the door closed behind him, the patients began breathing, and chatting, as the ward sprang back to life.

I lay back, and practised my routine with the coins.

"That's rather good," the ward doctor said, as he looked at my charts and x-rays.

"Thank you," I said. "I have an audition on Thursday."

The doctor looked over the top of his glasses at me.

My heart sank. "Or rather… I did have an audition on Thursday. I assume I'm not going to make it?"

"Well, you never know…" The doctor said with a grin. "Perhaps somebody could fetch you a magic wand, and say abracadabra? Otherwise, you will have to wait for those bones to stitch themselves together the old fashioned way.”

That night, and the next day, were long, painful, and lonely.

I lay on my bed, watching the ceiling fans, devising challenging sequences of effects, using the few coins I had to hand. There were some nice chains of two or three effects that worked well together. I was experimenting with which chains fitted well together into a routine, when Harry visited.

She marched into the ward, with a teddy bear under one arm, and a Rocshelle’s hamper under the other. Her smile was thin, her cheeks streaked with tears. “Simon?”

“Harry!” I sat up as best I could. “Are you okay?”

“Am I…?” She perched on the edge of the bed. “I’m fine! Of course I’m fine! Although, I just had a visit from the police, and they say somebody beat you up? And said something about Danny? And…”

“A very angry Scotsman said that Conrad Drake sends his regards, whoever that is.”

"I have no idea!" She smiled a little. "You look…terrible."

"Ah." I waved a dismissive hand. "I feel worse. Is Danny okay?"

"He's in Monte Carlo, on business," she said. Her smile flickered. "Well, there was a business meeting somewhere in the month. He would call the rest of it research."

"Ah." I looked at the hamper. "You didn't have to do that."

"This?" She put it on the bedside table. "This is literally the least I could do. I just grabbed it from the warehouse." Her expression faltered and sagged. "I'm sorry. I have no idea what this is about, or where it is from, but the idea it's something to do with us, that I might be responsible? I'm so sorry."

I put a hand on hers. "You didn't do this. And you didn't have to come here to apologise. I know you have your own life to live."

"I came to check you were okay." She flushed. "I kept meaning to write, to catch up, and make good as a friend, but there was always something to do, and I could never find the words, and then I worried I had left it too long, and then this happened and…"

I squeezed her hand. "I'm going to be fine. In a few days I will be home."

"You can't work like that!" She whispered.

"It's fine," I said, gently. "I can work something out." I glanced at the hamper. "Is that shortbread? Maybe we should bribe the nurse for a cup of tea, eh?"

We drank tea, ate some shortbread, and talked a while, catching up with each other's lives. My troubles with Al didn't seem to compare to her troubles with the company's board of directors. They wanted her in what she described as a vanity post, with a salary and a title, but no actual responsibility or influence.

She sipped her tea. "I'm being paid to sit on my hands and let the men in pinstripes do everything."

"A hard life?" I asked.

She sighed. "Actually, yes. Their proposals are all stripping the shop back to a profit margin and efficiencies, which I understand, but they don't take the human factor into account. They don't think about why it is the shopper trusts the advice of a good salesman, or how offering a better service might make a little less profit on the one item you sell, but will ensure the customer comes back, every time." She looked at the hamper. "They want to profit from the name and reputation of the store, but it took my grandparents a long time to build that reputation, and it is only worth a penny, as long as we live up to it."

"And this is the moment that your brother took to go play blackjack somewhere?"

Harry chewed her lip. "He did this. He wants the money. So… he pulled the pin out the grenade, tossed it at me, and ran. He is going to be laying doggo until the dust settles."

"And there's nothing you can do?"

She flushed. "Not unless your Scotsman finds him. Father was… a little old fashioned. Oh, he was always proud of my work in the store, but not as proud as he was going to be when I grew up, and got married, and didn't need a baby-substitute to fill my time anymore. He made sure Danny got the lion's share of the power and the influence." She sniffed. "See? You didn't need this mess in your life, did you? I can already see your eyes glazing over."

"No." I raised an eyebrow. "I think you really needed to let some of this out over a pint."

"Somehow I doubt they have a bar here," she said, her smile warming, "so maybe we should worry about that another time. Is there anything you need? Clothes? A book?"

I flushed a little. "You have already been too kind."

"Nonsense." She patted my knee. "I'll get a care package put together, and will have somebody drop it of tomorrow. Hopefully, in a few days, we can have that drink. If you want to repay my kindness, keep your promise to let me talk things through."

It seemed like a fair deal. I readily agreed.

Eight

Harry kept her appointment for the drink.

She was waiting for me when I was discharged, and we took a brisk walk to the nearest pub. I bought a round, while she claimed us a table, near the fireplace. When I set the drinks down, she leant across the table. "How does it feel to be free?"

I rubbed my cheek. "Mostly brilliant, but a little scary. I can't work like this, and I missed my auditions. I've been trying not to think about how to make ends meet."

Harry looked away. "I wish I could help. Once upon a time I would have been able to find you a job at the store, but these days I don't think I could, without Danny signing the paper, and…" Her words trailed off. "Sorry. I can't."

I looked at her. "What is it?"

Harry forced herself to smile, but her eyes were heavy with troubles. "He was meant to be in touch by now. Last night I received a telegram, telling me he was headed to Venice for a while. There was no address, or contact details. No hint he might actually come back and see his grand plan being achieved, or… or… if it will all fall to cinders around us."

I took her hand. "Is it so bad?"

She swallowed. "As far as Danny would be concerned, it is going to be a roaring success. For the next couple of years, it will make a wonderful profit, but it will not be the store I knew, and it will not last." She sipped her beer, and toyed with her hair. "The store I know might be a little old fashioned, but it has survived because it has always had its own identity. The world changes. We embrace those changes, and cater to them, but we are always Rochelle's. The board believe they can see where the world is turning to, where the changes will come, and are planning to be the icon of that fashion, but… when that tide ebbs, they will have nowhere to go. To Danny it wont matter. We will have made our money, and whatever is left can be sold off. He thinks it will last a few decades, but I imagine the changes will come about far sooner. There are ideas he, and father, would laugh off and belittle that have far, far greater momentum than either would believe." She closed her eyes. "At least Father would have seen that. He would have wanted to make the decision himself, but he would have listened to me!"

"You miss him," I said quietly, "don't you?"

"Every day." Harry choked on a bitter laugh. "I don't know if I want to grab him into a hug, and never let go, or slap the stupid bugger for getting himself killed, but... I would do anything to see him again. Especially now."

I held myself back from the obvious question. It burned in my throat, determined to ask.

"It was a car crash," she said, quietly. "Just like it said in the papers. It was the early hours, raining, and he was on his way home from his club. He lost control. They said it would have been almost instant. Too quick for him to suffer." Her lip trembled, and her voice wavered. "The newspapers didn't report that he was completely pickled. I don't think it fooled anybody."

I nodded. "I'm sorry."

Harry gave me a sad smile. "You didn't have anybody to visit you in hospital?"

I shook my head. "Mum and Dad both died in the war. Dad was aboard the HMS Hood when it went down. Mum was caught in air raid."

Harry pursed her lip. "I'm sorry."

"I had been evacuated long before then," I whispered. "I was taken in a teacher at a boarding school in the depths of the countryside."

Harry laughed. "A history teacher? Is that how you knew so much about Willow Lake?"

"Professor Lintwood," I said. "Lord alone knows what he did to deserve being lumbered with a miserable nuisance like me. He was… wonderful though. He was made entirely from kindness and patience. I did nothing to deserve either."

Harry tapped her glass to mine. "They should have sent you to my school. My Classics tutor could have done with a bit of a nuisance in their life." She looked at me. "What will you do?"

I sipped at my pint of ale. "I'll find something. There'll be an audition, or I'll find some work, one way or another."

We drank, and talked, for a while, but eventually I had to brave returning to my flat. I couldn't face going back to the lock up. Harry escorted me home, and helped me into my living room chair. She set the radio to warm up, and put the kettle on. I caught her snooping a little look around. Her smile was paper thin, and I could see the judgements behind it.

I shuffled through my missed post. The letter from Doris was mixed amongst the bills.

Harry poked her head around the door. "Well, this isn't what I expected."

"What did you expect?"

"Rabbits... a top hat... maybe one of those boxes they keep a mummy in..."

"That's all in my lock up," I said.

Her eyes flashed bright. "Really?"

I shook my head.

She sighed. "And I thought you would be fun. Well, this is…."

"Poky?" I suggested.

"Homely," Harry decided. "Modest but comfortable." She rubbed the back of her neck. "It was nice to see you again, but I have to… I have appointments."

"Of course." I shook her hand. "If I can ever help?"

She nodded. "You could ask me for another drink. We could talk some more." She handed me a business card. "Please? I could do with a friend."

"Then you have one," I promised.

Harry kissed my cheek. "Good! I like friends!"

*

The letter from Doris was a troubling read. There had been arguments with her boyfriend, little things that he wouldn't let go of, even if he knew he was wrong. The final word he always had to have. Little things that had once seemed cocky and smart, now just seemed petty and rude. There was hope, and joy, too, but they were worn thin and half hearted.

I read the letter several times, trying to decide if the small stain that smudged one corner was that of a tear.

When I fell asleep, the words of the letter echoed in my dreams.

*

A few days later, having given up on rest, I was in my agent's office. Tony was an impish fellow, with receding hair and weary eyes.

He gestured at me over the mess of papers on his desk. "You want to audition looking like that? Is it hurting you to stand there?"

"Only when I breathe," I said. "I'll heal. The bruises will go down, before a pantomime is out of rehearsal. I just want to avoid starving, or being evicted. There must be something? Anything?"

"I have some stores that want a Father Christmas, but

they want somebody older, and…" Tony gestured at my face. "Maybe to look a little less like he fell out the sleigh?"

"Tony, please, is there anything?" I asked.

He gave me a sorry look. "There's one option, but you won't like it."

My heart sank. "You want me to sell my tricks?"

"A few of them. I can find a buyer for Strange Bedfellows and The Goldfish."

I shook my head. "The holiday camp said they wanted me back for the next season! What would I perform?"

"Something else!" Tony chuckled. "You know that two thirds of the Professor's routine is far too good for a camp. It deserves to be on stage."

"Then get me a stage?" I pleaded.

Tony snipped the end off a cigar, and leant back in his chair. "I've had enquiries."

"From whom?" I asked.

Tony lit the cigar. "Saxon."

Saxon was a Headliner, who had a reputation for

swooping on other acts, to buy out the tricks and effects that would then become 'his'. Saxon mostly performed on stage, but had been in cinema serials, feature films, and a long running radio drama.

I drew a breath. "Tony, you told me I had to keep the acts, because one day, when I was on stage, they would be my goldmine."

Tony shrugged. "I thought you would be there by now. You aren't. Now is the time to consider other options."

An awareness of my bills weighed heavy on my shoulders. "Just those two effects?"

Tony puffed on his cigar. "For now. Perhaps opportunity will knock again."

My chest fell tight, and my head span. I made myself nod. "Very well. Make the arrangements."

NINE

I hopped off the bus at the end of the street, with a satchel full of groceries. I had fallen into the habit of hurrying towards home, by slowing down and being careful. If I marched off at my usual speed I would be forever stopping, to nurse my side and catch my breath.

My flat was on the fifth floor of a Victorian building, whose grandeur had faded over the decades. There was a motorbike parked by the steps. The sight of it set my heart racing, even before my brain realised it was Doris's bike.

I lumbered up the steps, making haste with less speed, and scaled the mountain of staircases to the fifth floor. Somewhere, beyond the rush of adrenaline, my bruises screamed in complaint and stabbed at me.

I emerged from the stairs into the hallway, and froze.

Doris was sat by front door, reading a paperback novel. She glanced up at me. In the first instant I wanted to grin like an idiot, rush over, and sweep her into a hug, to laugh and hold her. In the next instant anger and sadness ripped at my heart.

She had a black eye.

Doris stared back at me. "What… what happened to you?"

"I wrote to you," I said. "I… was jumped at my lock up. Never mind me! What is that?"

Doris looked at the floor. "We had a fight. I walked out. He did this, to try and make me stay. I kicked him in the happy sacks, and left anyway." She gestured to a rucksack stuffed with clothes. "I didn't have anywhere else to go. I hoped maybe you have a spare room? Or a sofa?"

I unlocked my front door. "You can have my room. I'll take the sofa."

Doris followed me into the flat. "What do you mean you were jumped?"

I held up my hands. "Okay. We both need to talk about this. How about we do it over a cup of tea."

She grinned, and shoved me. "I thought you would never ask!"

Harry found a record in my collection that she approved of, and dropped the needle, while I poured the tea. Her old smile was back on her face, as she leant on the counter in my kitchen, and watched me preparing the meal.

"What is it?" She asked, a little unsure.

"Cassoulet," I said. "It's French. It will take a few hours to cook slowly, but it will be worth the wait."

Doris raised an eyebrow.

"It's a casserole," I said.

"Oh." She shrugged. "Well, I'm game to try it."

I glanced at her bruised eye. "He really hit you?"

"It will be the last time," she assured me. "Although, precisely what I'm going to do now? I have no idea. I hear there's a fruit and veg firm who are down a workman, maybe I could do that?"

I didn't fancy her chances of convincing anybody at the

depot that she could do what they considered a man's work, regardless of how many circles she could have run around Al. "We will find you something, and with a little luck, money won't be a problem in a few days."

Doris stepped around me, and looked at the hamper. "You've been seeing Harry?"

I made a brief explanation of my beating, and how Harry found me in hospital.

Doris frowned at me. "Well, if that's all it took for her to remember you…"

I rolled my eyes. "She tried to be a good friend."

Doris gave me a playful shove. "What? She managed to resist your obvious sexual magnetism?"

I waved a carrot at her. "Don't. It isn't like that."

"I know." Doris took the carrot from my hand. "Isn't that the problem?"

"No." I cocked my head. "It just… isn't meant to be."

"Ah." Doris prodded me with the carrot. "So, you are giving up?"

"No." I smiled. "I'm adjusting to what she needs, and trying to be a good friend in return."

Doris stepped behind me, put her arms around me, and her head on my shoulder. "Well, I appreciate you being a good friend. I hope she does too."

*

That night I lay on my sofa, staring at the ceiling, trying to sleep.

Doris was snoring like a steam locomotive struggling on a steep hill. Her nasal tones echoed around the flat, filling every nook and cranny.

Eventually, around three in the morning, I rose and made myself a coffee. As the percolator stuttered and sputtered on the hob, I leant over the sink, and stared out the kitchen window, over the back of the building.

Somebody stood in the alley, watching the building. They pressed themselves into the shadows, but I got a fleeting impression of a wide brimmed hat, and a shapeless overcoat. They turned and hurried away in a heartbeat. The shape was wrong for the man who assaulted me, too small, too slender, and without the lumbering quality to his movement.

The surge of panic in my chest subsided to curiosity.

I made my coffee and drank at the kitchen table, deep in thought.

*

Doris sipped her cup of tea, and waved a slice of toast at me. "It wasn't the guy who did that to you?"

I shook my head. "I was more worried it might be the one who did that, to you."

"Oh." She touched her black eye. "Well, if it is, he best not let me see him."

We were at a greasy spoon café, halfway between home and the lockup. It was decorated in black and white tiles, the windows fogged in condensation.

I poked my breakfast with a fork. "Do you have any plans for today?"

Doris groaned. "I suppose I better start looking for

work."

"I don't suppose," I said, softly, "you want to help me out?"

Doris smiled. "I get to be a beautiful assistant to a magician?"

"More… a business partner. I have to sell some tricks. I need to prepare the props and instructions. I could use an extra pair of hands, and when I get paid… I'll pay you?"

"So…" She looked at me. "You make props for others now?"

"No." I rubbed the back of my neck. "Since I can't work, I'm selling Effects. Not just the props, but… the idea, and the right to perform them."

"Oh." She hesitated. "Sounds serious."

"I'm doing what I can to stay afloat, and with a little luck I can replace them with something new before the summer." I gave her a guilty look. "The thing is, my manager Tony, didn't think to arrange the meeting at my lockup. I have to get the materials to Saxon's workshop."

"Saxon?" Doris perked up. "Mandrake Saxon?"

I nodded.

Doris gave me one of those looks that stirred butterflies in my chest, the one that was playful and teasing, but without any hint of spite, or a trace of malice. "Well… you did offer me sanctuary, and buy me breakfast…I think I can help out."

We finished breakfast and walked to the lock up.

I walked to the door, and froze. I looked around, checking and doublechecking the corners and shadows. My chest tightened in a way that it hadn't since I was in the service, since the last time I went on patrol in Malay.

"Simon?" Doris put her hand on my arm. "Are you okay?"

I nodded and let us into the lock up.

Doris stepped past me, and into the tunnel, inspecting my shelves of tricks. She reached for the Singing Sword. "What's this?"

"Something I was working on for my routine." I lifted it off the shelf and took a few swings, thumbing the stud in the grip that set the mechanism running. The sword whistled a low, mournful song, a lament. "There is a channel in the blade. The chisel edge at the mouth moves to change the note."

Doris grabbed another box from the shelf. She pointed to the label. "My pet ghost?"

"Another work in progress." I shoved the box back.

"Can I see it?" She asked, with a smile that made it hard to refuse.

"We don't have time for me to demonstrate every trick on the shelf," I said. "Sorry."

"But…" Doris stared straight into my eyes. "You could maybe show me one?"

I nodded and shrugged off my overcoat, and put on the jacket from the box, over my roll necked sweater, and began the routine. I took the silk handkerchief from the breast pocket of the jacket, and showed it to Doris, before screwing it up so small I could conceal it in my closed fist. When I opened my fist and flicked out the handkerchief, it had appeared to grown to the size of a bedsheet (its shapeless billowing disguising the swap for the sheet whipped out of my sleeve).

Doris was polite enough to clap. "Is this how you change your bed?"

I flicked my wrist. The bedsheet billowed into the air once more, then wallowed slowly downwards. Instead of crumpling to the floor, it seemed to hang, draping over a solid form, taking the shape of a simple Halloween ghost, floating a little above the floor.

I stepped back, and the ghost followed me, bobbing with the movement.

Doris squealed with delight. "A pet ghost!"

I gripped the sheet by the corner, and gave it another flick, releasing the valves on the inflatable segments, and reducing it back to a sheet, and detaching the fine wire that connected it to my sleeve. I folded it up, and put it to one side. I could replace the gas cylinder and reset the mechanism later.

I took the drawings and notes for the Strange Bedfellows, and the Goldfish from my safe, took their boxes off the shelves, and stowed them into luggage cases for transport.

"Is that everything?" Doris asked.

"No. Some of the props have flash paper. I store them nice and safely." I unlocked the strongbox.

"Oh, hey…" Doris picked up my coin-launcher. "What is this?"

"Be careful!" I took it from her. "It was meant to make coins appear with a little style, but it needs work."

"Why?"

I grinned, and rolled up my sleeve, to strap the device on the underside of my wrist. I primed it with a coin, and rolled my sleeve over it. I aimed it at my safe, and flicked my wrist.

The coin shot down the length of the lockup and struck the safe with a chime.

Doris tapped her lip. "I can see the problem. Maiming

the audience is not advised." She looked up and saw the coins in the ceiling. "You should be carefull with that!"

"It needs work," I agreed. "Come on, we'd better get a hurry on. I don't think Saxon likes people being late."

I locked up, and we carried the luggage case between us, to the bus stop.

TEN

'Mandrake Saxon' was the stage name of one Malcolm Crawley, a slick, matinee idol of a man, well groomed and smartly turned out man, who favoured dark suits and a bowtie that always suggested, without being, the uniform of a classical magician in a dinner jacket and top hat.

His workshop was housed in a vast yellow brick building on the banks of the Thames, that had been a paint factory in my youth. There, as well as his own tricks and effects, his team built a variety of props, and sets with concealed effects, for stage and screen. It had become very fashionable for shows in the West End, especially in Panto season, to boast some cunning illusions and dazzling effects with his fingerprints all over them.

Our first glimpse of him was from the floor of his workshop, as he loomed overhead, on a catwalk gantry, to his office. He was smoking a pipe, and staring down at the many different props, sets, and other objects, around the vast workshop floor, and the small army of skilled artisans in constant motion, as they toiled away.

Doris spotted him, and nudged me.

"Harry!" Saxon shouted down to the foreman, who was guiding us through the chaos. "Is that the Professor?"

"Aye!" Harry said, doffing his flat cap.

Saxon leant over the railing for a better look at us. "Send them up!"

"Well did the stupid sod think I was going to do?" Harry grumbled, waving us towards the stairs. "This way."

We climbed the spiral staircase to the catwalks, and followed the main walkway in the direction of the circular glass office, from which Saxon was said to see all, and know all, that went on in his domain.

I looked over the side, down upon the patchwork of distinct sets. A cave in an exotic desert rubbed shoulders with the banquet hall of an ancestral mansion. A little way away, a group of men were struggling with the head and neck of a dinosaur, or dragon, of some sort.

Doris clung to my arm. "Do you think he could be free for the summer?"

I gave a look of mock pain. "You wouldn't miss me?"

"He has a dragon!" Doris whispered. "You have cards and coins." She rocked on her feet and pointed at the banquet hall set. "And a suit of armour! You could use a suit of armour!"

Saxon marched over to meet us. "He used to have one, when he was that godawful clown. What was his name? Mucky?"

Doris beamed. "Muddles? He still is Muddles." She looked at me. "You never told me you knew Mandrake Saxon!"

I flushed. "I don't. We met once, and it was purely business."

Saxon waved us into his office. It was fashionably decorated, the desk covered in paperwork and designs, all neatly stacked and ordered. On the wall, between the many windows, were framed posters from his stage shows and movies.

He opened a drinks cabinet, and poured himself a cordial, without offering us one. "Ah! Muddles. He had a suit of armour once, but it was so cumbersome to carry to small engagements, and…What was the other thing?"

I groaned. "It required two assistants, that I don't have."

Doris looked at me. "So, you sold it?"

I gave her a sheepish look. "My career wasn't going anywhere, and I couldn't use the effect, so I thought… maybe this was a way to get me noticed."

Doris chuckled. "Was it any good?"

Saxon chuckled, and pointed to one of the posters, in which he was being menaced by the Clockwork Man. "It goes down well with my younger audience."

Doris squeaked.

"What?" I asked.

"I saw that trick!" She grinned at Saxon, turning scarlet. "I loved that trick. I had the wind up toy!"

She seemed incredibly proud of that fact.

Saxon smiled, politely, and gestured to our large case. "Might I see them?"

I handed him the papers first, then demonstrated the operation of the trick. Strange Bedfellows appeared to be a simple card trick, but as I shuffled the deck, I kept finding random objects (a pocket watch, handkerchief, some money, sweets, and even a pint of milk) in the deck, appearing them through a concealed mechanism.

"Ah!" Saxon smiled. "So, we could pick pocket our volunteer and find his own pocket litter in the deck? Wonderful. And the other trick?"

The Goldfish was a trick bowl in which a candle appeared to burn underwater, on the third attempt. The first attempt was the failure one would expect if you tried to light a candle underwater. The second attempt was foiled by the magic being too strong. The fish in the bowl (a fairly convincing puppet) 'turned to gold' in a flash of white hot flame.

The third attempt succeeded, convincingly.

Doris cooed excitedly, and clapped.

Saxon held up a finger to her. "You don't have to do that. The quality sells itself. I will have to dress them up, and add a little stagecraft to make them pop, but they are solid ideas. They are good ideas." He opened a drawer, and took out a chequebook and pen. "Congratulations. They are sold."

I took the offered cheque, and studied it. I wasn't rich, but I could fend the bills off for a while. I folded it away into my pocket.

*

The bus rumbled on. Doris took one of the few seats available, and I turned the empty case on its end to use as a seat. It swayed dangerously, but the conductor hadn't said anything, so I pretended not to notice his unimpressed looks.

"We should celebrate!" Doris said. "We could go out for a meal. I know a place!"

"Doris," I said, gently, "I have to pay you, then I have to make this last."

Doris pouted. "That plan is far too sensible for my tastes."

"Sorry," I mumbled. "I was planning to cook again?"

"Oh! A woman could get used to that!" She shoved me.

I grabbed the chair before I toppled away, which just made Doris laugh.

The bus slowed towards the corner.

I hopped up, and rung the bell. "This is us."

We carried the case between us, to the lockup. On the walk back to mine, Doris stepped in close, and slipped my arm about her.

"Are you okay?" I asked.

She let her head rest on my shoulder. "Sorry. I caught myself thinking."

"Anything I can…"

"No." She drew a breath. "I have spent all day trying to forget about him, because the thought of what happened the other day, of remembering the look in his eye when he decided to punch me, leaves me sick, it turns my stomach, but… I miss him. Or… I miss…"

"You miss who he let you believe he was," I said gently, "and hate the man he revealed himself to be?"

Doris hugged me close. "Everything I thought I had, everything I thought I he was, has all been poisoned, and it all means… nothing!"

"Oh." I held her close. "Did you… want to go for that meal? Maybe we could take your mind of things for a while?"

"No." Doris dragged her heels a little. "No, I couldn't do that. You're right. Times are lean, and you are in a state. We should have a quiet night in."

That plan went out the window as we crossed the road to my building.

Harry was sat on the steps, smoking a cigarette, mesmerised by the motorbike.

Doris chuckled. "Huh. There appears to be a pretty

young woman waiting for you."

I nodded. "It's becoming something of a habit lately. Which… is new."

Doris laughed, and pulled herself free from me. "Hey! Harry!"

Harry leapt to her feet, and sprinted over to grab me in a hug, as she burst into tears. "Simon! I'm sorry. I didn't know who else to trust." She gripped my hand so tight I could feel her pulse. "Did you truly mean the promise to be my friend?"

I cupped her cheek. "What's wrong?"

"Danny," she whispered. "I think he is in deep trouble. Can we talk?"

ELEVEN

We sat around the kitchen table, waiting for the tea to brew in the pot.

Harry took a manilla envelope out from under her jacket, and slid it across the table. Her eyes were full of tears, and she chewed on her lip, as I tapped the contents onto the table. There was a typed letter, and a pile of glossy photographs.

The photographs were of a window, into a bedroom, in which Danny, and another young, athletic, and painfully handsome man, were indulging in their most carnal desires. I flicked through them quickly.

Doris arched an eyebrow, and gave Harry a sympathetic smile.

Harry reached over and held out the letter.

I ran my eyes over it, and read aloud: "Harriet Rochelle. I am not only aware of, but as you can see, have undeniable proof of your brother's vices. These photographs are a small selection from a far larger collection, that are a comprehensive catalogue of the partners whom Daniel has enjoyed, on his yacht, in various hotels, and his London apartment. It is in my power to distribute these photographs in such a way as to ensure a scandal that would not only destroy Daniel's life, but those of his fellow deviants. I am, however, willing to surrender the entire collection and the negatives, for a reasonable price of five thousand pounds. Rooms have been booked at the Ash Tree Inn, at Whitt, in Scotland, for this Thursday, with onwards travel arrangements made for the next morning. It would be in nobody's best interest for either the authorities, or your company board, to become aware of these arrangements, and I advise against you betraying the trust in which you are currently held. Yours Sincerely, Conrad Drake."

Doris took the letter from me, and read it herself. "This is…"

"Blackmail," Harry said, quietly. "I disagree with my

brother, on a good many things, but I would never want to see him ruined." She drew a breath. "And whatever you think of these pictures…he is…"

Doris flashed her a disarming smile. "Oh please! I've never found that to make anybody more or less decent than I already knew them to be." She placed the letter on the table and tapped it with her finger. "Bullies, bigots, and blackmailers on the other hand, I tend to have a problem with. So… how do we get word to the Police, without these people knowing, and without the Police poking their nose into Danny's bedroom business, where I can't see any reason for them to belong?"

Harry sighed. "I don't see we can. Danny might find a way, but Danny, if I could reach him, if I knew *how* to reach him, would want to be loyal to his friends. He would pay to protect them." She rubbed the back of her head. "I believe I should. If I can obtain those photographs and destroy them…"

Doris softened her voice. "Harry, a bully doesn't give

up their grip on you so easily. Once they know you are willing to pay, they will know it is because you *have* to pay, and they will always want something. They will have a hold of you, and they will not let you go."

Harry stared into the distance, deep in thought. "Then I will have no choice, but to hope they approach their business as professionals rather than bullies."

Doris pointed at me. "So far, Conrad Drake seems very much to be a bully!"

I nodded. "These are dangerous. Maybe we should try and think of a way to¬"

Harry shook her head. "They know I would never risk that. I have to go. I just don't think I can go alone." She stared at me. "I was wondering if the Professor could accompany me, and keep his eyes open for trouble? Like you did for Doris, exposing that card cheat, back when we met?"

"This," Doris said, sharply, "is a little different!"

Harry nodded. "Yes, it is. The problem is, I have to go, if you help me or not, but I would feel much safer if you were watching my back."

I glanced at Doris.

Doris poured the tea. "She has a point. She is stupid enough to do this, whatever we do."

My heart sank. "Then I best do what I can to help."

"We!" Doris corrected me. "I'm coming too."

Harry's eyes widened. "You are? Why?"

Doris laughed. "Well, one of us should know how to handle themselves in a fight."

"Ah." Harry chuckled. "Well, she does have a point."

Doris squeezed my shoulder. "What? You keep your friend out of trouble, and I'll keep my friend out of trouble."

Doris did the butterfly-smile again.

"Okay," I said, quietly. "I guess we are doing this…"

Harry nodded. "Yeah. So… is there anything we need to prepare for this? Like, an emergency plan or something?"

I dug out my notebook and pencil. "Actually, I have some ideas."

"Me too!" Doris bounced on her heels. "Can I borrow

some of your stuff?"

*

I opened the lock up first thing in the morning, and Doris followed me in, wheeling her motorbike.

She set at the far end of the lockup, on its kickstand. She gave it a loving caress. "Will it be safe here?"

I took some of the chains and locks from the shelf. "Want these?"

She took them with a grin, and wrapped then through the spokes and around the forks. "From an escape routine?"

I nodded, stuffing the concealed pockets in my jacket with lockpicks, files, and a selection of tools from my workbench. There was a prop pipe in my pocket, which gave me an idea. I unlocked the strongbox, and took out the tobacco tin that held my flash and smoke bombs.

Doris leant past me for the coin launcher. "I'll take that."

"What?" I glanced at her. "That sounds a bad idea. That could mess somebody up."

"Yes," she said, strapping it on. "The shaved gorilla next time he tries to beat you up."

I closed the strongbox, before she had any other ideas. "Fair enough."

Doris squeaked in delight, and plucked something off my shelves. My Mrs Punch puppet. She put it on her hand, and made a few experimental gestures with it. "So... Harry came running straight to you?"

I cleared my throat. "As a friend."

"Right." She narrowed her eyes. "You aren't going to do anything stupid are you?"

"Other than escorting her to meet dangerous criminals?"

"Like..." She frowned a little harder. "You don't have any flowers concealed in there do you?"

"No!" I backed away. "No."

"Good!" Doris said, in a Mrs Punch voice.

I flicked the puppet on the nose. "Because, apparently, if I thought a girl liked me it would be terrible."

Doris shook her head. "Yes, because you would make a mess of it, or…"

I sighed. "Or trip over myself for somebody who isn't worth it?"

Doris winced. "Hey, about what I said that night. She doesn't exactly see the same stuff you see in her, but… what would I know? The first time I saw you, I thought you were an absolute numpty. And…" She touched the faded bruise, under her eye. "I guess maybe with my track record, I'm not exactly the expert opinion you should be trusting." She slouched against the workbench. "I probably shouldn't have said anything that night. I mean, most the time I knew you, I've been dating idiots, or having my heart torn to pieces, and…"

"And you have faced, head on, everything I am always terrified will happen, head on," I said, softly. "You have never let it dent your faith, or make you doubt yourself. You are always willing to see the best in others, and to trust your own heart. I am far, far, too cowardly to ever take the risk, to dare wonder what if somebody said yes, or was the right one." I looked down at my feet. "You are absolutely fearless, and it is… amazing."

Her shoulders sank. "That isn't a good thing."

"It's not?" I asked.

She shook her head. "It just meant that I wasn't afraid to fumble it with those guys. It means that they weren't the people I was afraid of losing, if I fumbled it, or if the passions burned out, or… if I made usual mess of it." She stared down at her feet. "There were some people I would never ask, because it turns out I'm not fearless, at all."

I stepped over and leant on the workbench beside her. "Harry is a good friend, but she never gave me the butterflies."

Doris leant against me, her head on my shoulder. "Huh. You really get the butterflies?"

"Sometimes," I admitted. "When the right person smiles at me, or when there's a… quality to her voice." I sighed. "I always assumed you would get the butterflies."

"I do," she said, quietly, "but not for that. Butterflies are for flings. That sounds much more like the fuzzy warmth. Like… a cosy blanket. All wrapped up and safe."

I nodded. "Oh, for me it is definitely butterflies."

She laughed. "But not for Harry?"

"No…" I felt my smile grow rosy and faltering. "No, friendship feels more like…"

"Being at home?" Doris suggested, snuggling closer.

"Yes," I whispered.

The cadence of her breathing changed. "These last few days, I thought everything was going to fall apart, and I thought I was going to break to pieces, but… I felt like I came home."

"And here I am," I said, "dragging you straight back into trouble."

"I don't mind," Doris said. "It's kind of… endearing really."

She was smiling.

I didn't have to look. I could feel it in the butterflies it gave me.

TWELVE

We left London on the sleeper train to Inverness, and from there, took the Highland Railway to the cost, before transferring onto a bus, to follow the nooks and crags of Scotland's northern most coast.

As I stepped off the bus, with Doris and Harry, we stood a moment by the sea wall, and looked out towards the horizon.

Whitt was a remote fishing village, a tiny spot, in a cove, easily overlooked and forgotten on maps. It was little more than a hamlet, a few tall and narrow cottages clinging to cliffside as the rolling moorland suddenly met the craggy, rocky, coast. At one end the village widened slightly to allow for a short, dead end street, with a post office, a pub (that grandly called itself a hotel) and a few other little buildings. There were two cars (a spritely three wheeled sportscar, and a luxurious saloon) parked by the hotel.

The harbour was box shaped, and contained a flotilla of small, sturdy, steam trawlers. A light house crowned the harbour wall.

Beyond, the harbour, on the horizon, a handful of rocky islands jutted out of the restless, slate grey waves. They were stark, unwelcoming islands, their cliffs and steeples of dark stone, crowned by tufts of rough grass.

Harry drew in a deep breath. "Shall we?"

A few brisk moments later, we stood in the small foyer of the hotel. It was old, and looking tired in the ways that fresh paint and new furniture could not quite disguise. The reception desk, and the small office behind were deserted.

To our left was a doorway through a bar, where a squat, rubber faced man with thinning hair busied himself behind the bar, and a cluster of fishermen, in warm sweaters and dark working clothes, gathered around the open fire, sipping pints of ale, and sharing the gossip of the day. Scattered about the other tables were three other men: A round faced, portly individual in pinstripes, quivering nervously behind his newspaper, a square jawed and aristocratic older man, dressed in a pearl grey suit and drinking a shot, and a skeletal young man, drawn and gaunt before his years, in a flannel shirt and buff trousers.

Harry rubbed her hands, and slapped the bell.

The chime echoed around us, and at once, the three men sitting alone snapped their attention to the reception. The rubber faced landlord sprang into action, running for the door, while wiping his hands on a cloth.

The floorboards overhead creaked and groaned, as somebody lumbered down the stairs.

My blood froze. It was the giant who had assaulted me outside my lockup.

"You," I muttered.

He smiled at me. "Me," he agreed. "Ladies."

Doris gave me a worried look. "Is he…"

I nodded.

"Hello!" The landlord said, cheerfully. "Are these the last of Mister Drake's friends, Mister Thorn?"

"They are indeed," the giant said, in a genteel tone.

The landlord picked the last two keys from the board behind the desk, and tossed them the giant.

Thorn dangled them from his fingers, and loomed over the three of us. "I will show you to your rooms."

Doris tensed, her fingers curling into a fist. Her jaw set.

Thorn smiled at her. It was a cold, dangerous, smile. "If you would follow me."

Harry cleared her throat. "I don't suppose you could be a darling?" She pointed at the cases. "I'm afraid my friend has an injury. He would struggle."

Thorn took the three cases with ease, and lumbered up the stairs. We followed.

"You are up on the third floor," Thorn said. "The women will share the twin room. You will eat, in the dining room, at seven. You will be in your rooms by eleven, with lights out at eleven fifteen. You will be dressed, and in the lobby, ready to leave, at five o clock sharp. Your luggage will remain in your rooms. You will wear no hats, and carry no handbags, canes, umbrellas, or purses. You will not leave Whitt before that time, for any reason." He opened the first door, and waved Harry and Doris in. "On your pillow, you will find a playing card. To protect the identities and privacy of our *guests* you will not use your names, or suggest clues to each other's identities. From this moment, you will refer to each other by the name of your cards. I advise you not to try and deduce each other's identity. Mister Drake would not like it, which means I would have to… dissuade you." He dropped Harry's case on the nearest bed. "You are now the Queen of Clubs." He dropped Doris's case on the next bed. "You are the Queen of Diamonds." He marched across the narrow landing to the next room, and dropped my case on the single bed. "Joker."

I held out my hand. "My key?"

Thorn shook his head. "I will keep the keys."

He turned and lumbered away.

I walked to my window and stared out. I had a good view of the ocean, and the islands.

A flash of light caught my eye.

It was there and gone in a blink. A spark of reflected light on the largest island, amongst the reedy grass that topped the cliffs. Perhaps, I thought, from the lens of a camera, or binoculars.

I drew my curtains, and sat on the bed.

*

That evening we gathered in the dining room behind the bar, around a single long table. Thorn sat at the head of the table, with Harry, myself, and Doris along one side, the aristocrat, the portly fellow, and the gaunt young man, on the other. The meal was a reasonable fish pie, and garden vegetables.

Thorn raised his glass. "Ladies, gentlemen, would you care to place your cards on the table, so you might know how to properly address each other."

"M-may we talk at all?" The gaunt man asked.

Thorn nodded. "As long as you do not compromise each other's privacy."

The portly fellow laughed. "Well, does anybody know the football results?"

I placed my joker on the table. The aristocrat was Jack of Spades, the portly man the Ace of Hearts, and the gaunt man was the Seven of Diamonds.

"Well, I say!" Jack said, with a light, throaty, laugh. "I feel a little undone now. I couldn't have been a king?"

Harry smiled. "Are you a Jack-The-Lad?"

"Or Jack the Ripper?" Portly Ace asked.

The others laughed a little, and the air cleared.

Seven raised his glass. "Not bad for a poker hand."

Doris nodded, and they shared a small smile.

I settled into my meal, and tried not to be too obvious as I watched the others. Jack, I noticed, has an old school tie, and a regimental crest on his tie clip. Ace checked his pocket watch a few times, and compared it to clock on the wall, puffing his cheeks, and looking through the wall, into the distance. The watch was engraved, and although I could not see the words, I could make out the Masonic square and

Compass beneath them.

Seven offered me no clues to consider. There was a nagging feeling, when I looked at him, that there was something I should have noticed, but I couldn't put my finger on it.

After the meal most of the 'guests' went to the bar. I stepped outside for some fresh air.

Doris joined me, and we walked to the edge of the sea wall.

There was a fresh breeze, cold with spray, blowing in from the jet black waves. The islands stood out against the full moon. Thorn stepped outside, and lit himself a cigarette.

Doris took my hand in hers. "So, what are you thinking?"

I lowered my voice. "That it's rather odd, that of everybody at the table, Mister Thorn is watching us."

Doris shrugged. "We might be about to do a runner, or signal somebody."

"Perhaps," I whispered.

She smiled. "Or…"

"Or?" I asked.

Doris flushed. "Well, he doesn't know we are just friends."

We laughed, and she shoved me.

When she stopped laughing I found myself unable to look away from Doris, from her smile, and from the way she toyed with her hair.

"What?" She asked.

"I… like your smile."

"Oh?" She asked, half teasingly. "You aren't going to say something stupid, are you?"

"Only…" I looked away. "Only that when you wrote your letters, I could always tell when you were smiling, really smiling, as you wrote. There were little turns of phrase, and your sentences got longer, like they would never end, and…"

"And?" She asked.

"I felt the same butterflies," I admitted.

"Oh," Doris said, her smile fading, and her eyes widening. "I don't think I was ready to hear that."

"Sorry," I muttered. "I didn't mean to make anything difficult for you, it's just…"

"No!" Doris caressed my cheek. "I understand. This is the most excited, and scared, I have ever been. I know you love me. I know why you had to admit it now, before we… might let those words go unsaid. I even… hoped to hear them. I just… I'm not ready. Yet."

She leant close, and her lips brushed mine, in a kiss that sent shivers to my spine. Her breath, and her taste, lingered on my lips as she withdrew.

Doris paused, and leant against me, her head on my breast. "Oh. She whispered. Butterflies." Her breath softened. "Tell me again in a week. If I'm not ready then, tell me in another… In the meantime, just be… you."

PART THREE

LABYRINTH

THIRTEEN

At five the next morning we gathered in the reception, under Thorn's watchful eyes. He stood by the front door, his arms folded, and his jaw set.

Ace was the last to join us, waddling slowly down the stairs, his face sagging and his shoulders slouched under the sheer weight of the early start. Jack was dapper in dress, but sallow in his expression. Seven was sleepwalking. Doris and Harry were huddled together, chatting to keep each other's spirits up.

Thorn pulled the door open, letting the biting cold wind howl in. "This way."

We followed him out into the darkness, and he guided us to the harbour, where a small but hardy motor launch was waiting, the engine thrumming away, as it occasionally belched diesel smoke over the choppy sea.

Ace spluttered, and stared at Thorn, aghast. "You must

be bloody joking!"

Thorn waved to the iron ladder embedded in the stone of the harbour, the rungs slippery with weed and slime. "Please, Ace."

The rotund businessman shook his head. "And if I don't?"

Thorn smiled. "Then Mister Drake will make good on his promise."

"I'll help you," I said, climbing down, onto the boat. "Here."

The boat rocked and swayed underfoot, but I helped guide Ace down, and coaxed him into letting go of the rungs, and taking that final step down. He slumped onto the bench, and puffed out his cheeks.

"Buggering Hell!" Ace growled.

Jack crouched at the top of the ladder, and insisted on helping Harry and Doris down to join us. I took Harry's hand, and helped her step down. Doris jumped down, and landed in my arms, making the boat rock beneath us.

"Stop that!" Ace pleaded.

"Sorry!" Doris perched on the other side.

Seven hopped down swiftly, with the air of a practised seaman. If I was a betting man, I would put good odds on his having served in the navy.

Jack joined us, and Thorn was the last to board, casting us off, and taking his place at the controls. He opened the throttle, and swung the small wheel, pointing us towards the open sea and the islands. We bounced and rocked as the boat carved a path through the waves.

We swung about the islands, then approached the largest from the far side.

Lights flickered to life in the island, one at a time, burning behind windows, casting away the shadows from a building that rose out of the long grass. There were suggestions of gargoyles and cloisters, suggesting an abbey or cathedral as much as a manor house. As we grew closer, the scale of the building became apparent. It was a sprawling collection of wings and extensions.

Doris clutched my hand, as her breath was stolen.

Ace sat up a little. "Should we not be slowing?"

The manor house passed out of view, as we approached the cliff.

Ace went rigid, his eyes like flint. "Surely we have to slow?"

Doris leant against me. I put an arm around her.

The cliff filled the sky now. It was all we could see. And still we roared on.

More lights blazed suddenly illuminating a lightning bolt shaped wound in the cliff, glowing bright within the cave. Thorn slightly adjusted our course, to bring us in, barely missing the edge of the cave. Within was a natural cove, into which a dock had been built. We skimmed alongside, and Thorn killed the engines. He tossed a rope up onto the wharf, where another man, a bald, heavily scarred, man, in a butler's uniform, was waiting to tie the boat off.

"Up the ladder," Thorn commanded.

Jack led the charge, and we were soon up the ladder,

where the scarred man was waiting, armed with a shotgun.

"This," Thorn said, sharply, "is Mister Butler. You will follow his instructions and orders at all times."

Mister Butler gave us a long, appraising look, before nodding for us to follow him. "This way."

"To Drake?" Seven asked.

Butler cackled. "To breakfast."

We followed a narrow passage up a steep staircase. The rough rock of the cave gave way to smooth blocks of worked stone, as the lapping of waves was replaced with the song of the wind. The passage emerged into a vaulted cellar. Butler continued to lead us through, through the vaults and up more stairs.

We stepped into a hollow shell of a gutted building. An empty husk, of what might once have been the kitchen. Wind and rain howled through windows with no glass, and the open maw of a doorway.

A long string of electric lights hung near where the ceiling should have been, flowing in through one door (from the hollow shell of a corridor) and out through another (to shell of a dining room). I looked up, through the open hole where a ceiling and roof should have been, through three more floors of ruin. Strings of lights were pinned to the walls, circling the windows, moving slightly in the wind.

Doris took my hand.

Thorn ushered on, and we followed Butler through the maze of ruins. After some minutes walking we arrived at a door.

Butler opened the door, and ushered us into a cosy dining room, with a long table laden in platters of sausages, bacon, eggs, and toast, wine red walls, and animal skulls, mounted on the wall like a hunter's trophies. An electric heater glowed in the fireplace. Directly over the fireplace was a mounted tiger skull. Spaced around the walls were fittings that appeared to be old gas lamps, that glowed with the clean, consistent light of electric bulbs.

Each of the placemats on the table had a different playing card stamped into the leather, one for each of us.

"See!" Butler said, pointing with his shotgun for us to sit. "Breakfast!"

"Ha!" King dropped into one of the seats and snatched up a plate, that he proceeded to bury in bacon and toast. "This is more like it! How about you?"

Ace grimaced, and put a hand to his stomach. "Perhaps just a coffee, to… help settle things."

Seven took a seat, and tentatively put a few items on his plate.

Harry looked between us. "What do you think? Well… I'm game." She grabbed a plate, and assembled herself a hearty meal. "Come on!"

I took a seat, and poured coffee for myself, Doris, and Harry.

Doris looked around, uneasily, as she sat. "So… how is this room… not a ruin?"

Harry waved a forkful at her. "Oh! Good question!"

I got up and walked to the wall.

Thorn glared at me. "What are you doing?"

I stamped a foot, and was answered by a hollow thud. I knocked my knuckles on the wall, and again there was the dull echo of a hollow behind the wall. "Hardboard. We are in a box, in the house."

Doris smiled. "Well, that's clever."

Butler slammed the butt of his shotgun on the floor. "Quiet! All of you." He checked his watch. "Now…"

There was shrill, banshee howl, and the lights dimmed.

A light flashed and pulsed within the tiger skull.

The banshee howl faded. A deep, crackling, voice filled the room, the light within the skull pulsing and flashing in time to its words. "Good morning, ladies and Gentlemen. I trust I have your full attention? My name is Conrad Drake. I apologise for the security precautions you have had to endure. Each of you is aware of your own business with me, and you can each imagine the situation of my fellow clients. The first cost of our business is, above all else, is privacy. Which brings me to my first order. Ace of Hearts?"

Ace blanched, in his seat.

Thorn was around the table in an instant, a stiletto bladed commando knife in his hand. He slammed Ace's face into his placemat, and pinned him down, the blade pressed against the back of his neck, ready to perform a killing blow.

Everybody tensed, frozen on place. Under the table, Doris was tugging her sleeve back, to get a good shot from my coin launcher. Her eyes were hardened, her lips pressed together.

I could see her dilemma. If she hit Thorn, there was a good chance his reaction would kill Ace, and even if she forced him away, then there would be Butler, with his shotgun. I placed my hand over hers, and she took the pressure off the trigger.

"Yes?" Ace squeaked, staring at the tiger skull.

Conrad Drake's voice seemed to come from everywhere, from all directions. "You were warned of the consequences of going to the authorities. Yet you approached a Detective Inspector Plummer of Scotland Yard. Explain."

"I... didn't... please!" Ace wailed. "Please!"

"Explain!" Drake demanded, the eyes of the skull burning bright.

Ace sobbed. "He didn't believe me! He believes me a fool. He took no action!"

There was a long silence. Then at last Drake spoke. "Bring him to me!"

Concealed mechanisms clunked, and one of the wall panels opened, revealing an angular corridor, that seemed to slant at a disconcerting angle. Thorn dragged Ace from his chair, and frog marched him into the corridor.

The door slammed closed, behind them.

"Joker!" Drake said, the eyes of the skull burning. "You and your party will be next. You were familiar with the terms of the letter?"

I glanced at Harry. She nodded. I said: "Yes."

"And," Drake continued, "you will meet them?"

"Yes," I reported.

"Good," Drake answered. "Seven of Diamonds?"

"Yes?" Seven said, the words catching in his craw.

"You are familiar with the terms stated in the letter?"

"Yes." Seven seemed to have to make himself say the words, with considerable effort.

"Are you prepared to meet them?"

Seven was silent. He nodded.

"Are you," Drake repeated, "prepared to meet them?"

"Yes!" Seven hissed.

"Jack of Spades?"

"Yes," Jack answered in a droll tone.

"You are familiar with the expected terms?"

"Yes," Jack asked.

"You are able to meet them?"

"Yes, damn it, I am."

"Excellent," Drake said, his tone lightening. "Then you will not be kept long. Please eat, drink and be merry."

The lights rose to their normal level.

"Well?" Butler demanded. "Eat!"

Nobody seemed to have much of an appetite.

The concealed pattern clicked open, and Ace emerged,

sobbing, defeated, and emotionally broken.

Butler stared at me. "Well, don't keep him waiting."

FOURTEEN

The door closed behind us, as Harry, Doris, and I stepped into the strangely slanting corridor. The walls gradually sloped to one side at an increasingly alarming angle as we progressed. The floor and ceiling sloped uphill.

The lights flickered. There were more of the faux-gas lanterns, regularly spaced along the corridor, that dipped and flickered in unison.

We started walking down the corridor.

Doris took my hand. "Do they think you're Danny?"

I gave her a hint of a shrug.

Harry snorted. "Ugh. Why does everybody think I need a big strong man to make the decisions?"

A door ahead of us opened, into another chamber. This was bigger than the dining room, with walls that sloped and tapered. They appeared to be covered in slabs of stone, covered in hieroglyphs and pictorials. Ahead of us was a raised dais on which an open fronted sarcophagus, the inside lined in black velvet. Its cover laying on the floor where it had supposedly fallen.

Overhead there were alcoves with theatre lights in.

I ran my fingers over the wall. "Plaster on wood."

Doris studied the hieroglyphs. "These are pretty. Do they mean anything?"

I looked them over. Some of the symbols were real, most were just imagined in the same style, and none of them made a coherent message. I shook my head.

Harry walked into the middle of the room, and turned on her toes. "Hello? Are we going to talk? Or is this another game?"

I glanced at Doris. "Where's Thorn?"

Doris frowned. "I have no idea."

The door slammed closed behind us, with a loud thump, too loud. The lights grew dim, and a spotlight cast a perfect circle of white on the floor. Once again Conrad Blake's voice came from all directions. "Harriet Rochelle, step into the light."

Harry did as she was told.

The theatre lights blazed as bright as the sun. So bright we had to shield our eyes. The sarcophagus was caught in stark shadow by the dazzling light. A blanket of fog covered the dais, and tumbled down onto the floor.

A figure melted out of the sarcophagus, as tall as me, slender and sleek, poised and graceful, it too was little more than a silhouette against the white of the light. It stepped to the edge of the dais, and stared down at us. "Did you bring me five thousand pounds?"

Harry nodded. "It wasn't easy, not being able to carry a bag, but…" She took a roll of papers from a pocket inside her jacket. "Bonds with a value of five thousand pounds."

"Excellent." The figure on the stage beckoned to her. "Place it on the step of the dais."

Harry did as she was told, dropping the bonds into the pool of white fog.

Instantly the lights blinked out, plunging us into

darkness. There was a soft chatter of a mechanism. The lights flickered back on, to a comfortable level rather than a glare. The cool mist faded and drifted away, revealing a metal bowl, in which lay a thick manilla envelope, a small bottle of whiskey, and a book of matches.

Harry stared at the envelope. "Is this all of them?"

"Would you like time to check the negatives?" Drake asked. "And dispose of them?"

Harry nodded. She looked between Doris and me. "Do you mind?"

We turned and walked to the door. It opened nearly silently. We stepped outside, and waited. A few minutes later Harry followed us into the corridor. She was pale, cold, and shaking.

"Harry?" I asked, softly.

"It's done," she whispered, taking my arm.

Doris put a hand on her back, and guided her through to the dining room. She was trembling, as she sat at the table. Doris crouched by her, and held her hands. I gave her coffee.

Seven stared at her, unsure what to do with his hands.

Butler nodded at Seven. "Go on then."

Seven slowly rose to his feet, and walked into the corridor like a condemned man.

Some minutes later, he emerged, looking no happier.

Jack rose to his feet. "Well, I expect this is me?"

Ace stared at the door, long after it closed behind Jack. "Pompous inbred arsehole."

Butler snorted, and gestured with the gun. "No more of that talk."

Ace turned on Butler. For a moment he looked about to say something, his lip quivering, and anger burning in his eyes.

Butler smiled back.

Ace sighed, and prodded at some bacon with his fork. He muttered under his breath.

Harry leant against Doris, resting her head on Doris's shoulder. Doris held her close.

We waited.

The door opened, and Jack emerged. He rubbed his hands together, and looked around us. "Is that it? Everybody done? Can we be back to the pub in time for the bar to open?"

Ace looked like he wanted to complain, but he nodded.

The lights dimmed, and the eyes of the tiger skull glowed. Drake spoke out.

"Mister Butler, escort them to the harbour. Thorn will return them to the mainland."

Butler stood, and swung his gun around all of us. "You heard the man."

We stepped out of the dining room and into a crisp, breezy morning. We marched back through the mouldering husk of the once grand manor. We walked in a grim silence.

Doris clung to my arm, as we descended the stairway into the cellars. We hung at the back, following the others down. I slowed. Something was wrong. Less of a smell in the air, more a tang, that I could taste.

"Smoke?" I muttered.

Doris glanced at me, and nodded. She ground to a halt, and stared into the shadows of the vault. Her grip on my arm tightened. "Something moved!" She whispered.

I followed her gaze, staring into the shadows, and the inky darkness. Something moved, vanishing from sight down one of the other passages.

"Hey!" Butler grabbed Doris by her shoulder. "Keep up with the others!"

"But there's somebody there!" Doris snapped.

The others stopped and looked back at us.

Butler snarled. "The group stays together."

"Excuse me!" Seven said. "What's… burning?"

I sniffed. There was more than a tang of smoke in the air now.

The air got thicker, as we descended into the cave, until it stung our eyes, and made us choke. We could hear the roar of flames before we reached the doorway.

The boat was adrift in the cove, and ablaze, consumed by a heaving mass of gold and orange flames. A jet of flame danced in the engine bay. Thorn's giant form lay across the back of the boat, being eaten away by the inferno.

Butler sagged, his knees buckling for a moment. "Thorm?" He straightened. His face torn between sobbing despair, and absolute fury. He turned slowly, his face going purple as he did. He lunged through the group and grabbed me, throwing me down onto wet stone floor. "You! You did this?"

Pain seared through my body. All my bruised woke up, and welcomed some new friends.

Butler brought the gun up, his face creased into a sneer. His finger squeezed the trigger.

I rolled aside, as the blast peppered and dashed the stone where my head had been.

Butler stepped forwards, trying to adjust his aim. I reached up and caught the barrel. He kicked me back, and stamped on me, smacking hard against the floor.

Butler pressed the double barrel under my chin.

"Oi!" Doris held her arm out straight.

Butler glanced up at her.

Doris flicked her wrist and there were three metallic thuds, as three coins sprang from the launcher, and struck Butler, on in the nose, and one in the forehead. He staggered away from me, his eyes rolling into his head. He dropped and landed heavily on his knees.

Everything froze for a split second, before Butler raised the shotgun to his shoulder, and squinted into the sights, taking aim at Doris.

I dragged myself up and threw myself into a tackle, slamming into Butler. His shot went wild, echoing about the cave. We tumbled together across the wharf, through the sea spray, and rolled to the edge. I grabbed one of the rusting mooring rings, as the floor vanished beneath us, and hung on. Butler yelled, as he toppled over, cracking his head on the side of the burning boat, as he fell.

The waves swallowed him.

When he bobbed up to the surface, her was face down, and unmoving.

I looked between the others. "Help me reach him. If we have a rope, or…"

He was already drifting out of reach.

Jack and Seven pulled me up onto the wharf. I lay there panting.

Doris knelt, and wrapped me in a hug.

"He's gone," Harry said, finally.

Ace tugged at his lapels. "Good riddance if you ask me. Well done lad! Well done!"

"Well done?" I stared at him, numbed by the cold of the grave. My words tasted of ashes and cinders. "A man is dead."

Ace shrugged. "I thought it was well done."

FIFTEEN

I don't remember whose idea it was to return to the dining room. I followed the others in a dull fugue, guided by Doris, her hand on my back.

The dining room at least offered some warmth and shelter. Outside the wind howled.

Jack, and Harry were discussing ways to signal to the land for help.

Seven was stood in a corner, his brow furrowed in thought.

Ace lumbered about the room. He suddenly began to shout. "Hello! Hello! Are you going to talk to us?" He stood by the tiger skull, and patted it. "Hello? Drake?"

Harry glared at him. "Is that really a good idea? He just killed his own henchman and trapped us here!"

"What?" Ace scoffed, wheeling around to point at me. "He killed the yob! And... I am sure Drake will understand it was in self defence.”

Harry stepped closer to Ace, almost nose to nose with him. “You blithering idiot! I meant Thorn! The giant! Do you think we killed him and burned the boat?”

Ace backed away from her. “Well, you might have done! And I don’t think that Mister Drake should punish the rest of us, for your crimes!” He flustered, and bristled. “Besides, Mister Drake must have a way off the island!”

Jack brightened. “That’s true! He must!”

“If,” Doris said, “he hasn’t used it already, and if he doesn’t kill us before we can use it.” She squeezed my shoulder. “What do you think?”

I closed my eyes. I tried not to hear the thud of Butler’s skull hitting the gunwale of the boat, playing over and over, behind my eyes. “Yesterday I was sure I saw somebody watching us arrive in town, from this island. There was a flash of light reflecting off something. We can take these silver plates, and flash SOS to the town, or fishing boats.”

Jack nodded. “Yes! That will work. I’ll go and do it.”

"Not alone!" Harry said. "None of us should go anywhere alone."

Jack gestured to seven. "How about it? I watch your back, and you watch mine?"

Seven nodded. "Yeah. I mean… if one of us killed the big bloke, it had to be tubby or the triplets."

"Me?" Ace squawked.

"He left this room with you," Seven said, "and never came back. He wasn't there when I went to the pyramid room, so…"

"What?" Ace spluttered. "You think it was me?"

Doris held up her hand. "There was somebody else. I saw them in the cellar."

"Drake?" Harry asked.

Doris shrugged. "I didn't get a clear look. Did any of us get a clear look at him? Ever? Or… how he came and went from the room?"

Jack tapped his lips. "Maybe if we knew that, we could find his way on or off the island. Or something useful. He has to have a kitchen around here, and maybe there are some supplies, or a radio?"

Ace groaned. "Well, which are you going to do? Signal for help, or search the island?"

Doris gave me a look, gesturing with her eyebrows.

"What?" I asked.

"Hidden doors?" She said. "Fake fog? Don't you think you could look for a hidden door? Isn't that something that might be in your skill set? Drake had to come in and out of the room somehow."

"Oh, the corridor slopes upward. The floor of that room is several feet above this one. There is a trick step in the dais. When our payment was taken, Thorn was in a passageway, under the dais."

Ace snorted. "Oh? And where in your overblown green grocery did you learn that?"

"What?" Jack asked.

"Oh please!" Ace said, pointing at Harry. "The Queen over there is Harriet Rochelle. She was in all those photographs with her father. It doesn't take much to work out that he has to be Daniel Rochelle. Or that they are being blackmailed because he buggered his way around every club in London."

Harry flushed. "Can we not¬"

"Well, clever clogs," Ace continued, "the secret entrance is obviously in the sarcophagus. How else do you think Drake was got in and out the room?"

"You never saw Drake," I said.

"Erm," Harry whispered, "are you sure? Because I did?"

"I saw him," Ace persisted. He looked to Seven and Jack for moral support.

Seven broke the awkward silence. "Why? What do you think we saw?"

"A silhouette," I said. "A simple cloth puppet lit from behind. It blends into the lining of the sarcophagus until it moves forward. I once designed a trick like that, which let it look like I had transported myself in and out of a suit of armour. Somebody else has used it to leave us with no idea what Drake looks like….” I trailed of, as that train of thought picked up speed, and rattled towards a conclusion. “Oh…”

Jack leant over the table, and cleaned off a plate. “Well, either you find that other door, or you search the manor, and find the rest of Drake’s facilities that way. Whichever. Seven and I will go and signal for help.”

Harry stood, and wiped her hands. “I can help.”

Jack grinned. “Good. Seven can watch our backs.”

“Well?” Ace pushed on the wall panel, trying to open the door to the corridor.

I got up, and slipped my lockpicks out of my jacket’s inside pockets, and slid it down the near invisible gap between the door and the frame. I felt the latch, and levered it open. The door swung inwards into the corridor.

Doris stepped past me to walk into the corridor. I followed her, and Ace lumbered after us.

We hurried to the pyramid room, and I dropped to my knees by the dais.

Doris crouched beside me, and prodded at the step. "This was where we put the payment, and…" The step clunked a little. "There is a little give."

I felt around the step. "Thorn must have been able to open it. There must be…" I couldn't find a latch or toggle. I tried pushing the top of the step inwards. "Here we go."

A flap dropped open on the face of the dais.

Doris grinned. "That's how he took the payment."

I nodded and reached in the flap, and groped around until I found a small lever. I pulled it, and a hatch released in the top of the dais. Within was a ladder down to a crawl-way.

"Ah." Ace cocked his head. "So… shall we?"

"In a moment." I climbed onto the dais and felt the small channel that ran a few feet forwards from the sarcophagus, disguised as the gap between flagstones. I took my favourite leather tool roll from inside my jacket, and chose a screwdriver. Prodding down into the groove I felt a chain mechanism I pulled on the chain, and a mechanism clicked and clunked.

The shape of a man, peeled out of the sarcophagus, suspended from a thin pole, formed from a silhouette of velvet, and given by a sprung framework being pulled taut by a web of thin wires.

Doris looked at me. "Is that your suit of armour?"

I nodded.

Her eyes widened. "So it must be…" Her expression hardened. "No wonder he didn't want anybody to see him."

"Who?" Ace demanded.

I looked up to the theatre lights. There was a small viewport hidden amongst them. "Saxon!" I shouted. "Mandrake Saxon! Are you there?"

There was no answer.

Ace burst out laughing. "You must be bloody joking?"

Doris pointed at the crawl-way. "Well? Want to go and see?"

SIXTEEN

I hopped down into the crawl-way. After a couple of yards, once we were past the back wall of the pyramid room, it opened into a more comfortable corridor. There was a ladder up to a small platform, with the viewport between the theatre lights, and a control panel.

Doris, Ace, and I spent a few minutes inspecting the controls. There was a speaker, that could be toggled to listen in to the kitchen or corridor, controls for the lights, the fog machine, the effects, and door locks. There was a microphone for broadcasting to the dining room.

Doris pointed to one of the controls. "Kitchen slash dining room? There must be another hidden door."

I nodded. "Interesting."

Ace cleared his throat. "This looks expensive."

"It is," I muttered. "But, I assume you were fined thousands of pounds too?"

Ace nodded. "And I wonder how many other clients he has. How often he runs this routine."

Doris looked thoughtful. "Enough for Thorn to upset somebody by demanding more money? Maybe the blackmailer didn't like being blackmailed himself."

"Maybe," I agreed. It was a distinct possibility, but not one we had evidence for. "We should explore the corridor. It has to go somewhere."

"Agreed." Ace said. He glanced down the ladder. "After you."

I dropped to the corridor, and paused to listen.

Somebody moved close by, but I couldn't see them.

"Saxon?" I demanded. "If that's you, we can talk. Something has gone very wrong here, and we can clear it up, before the Police get involved."

Footsteps echoed around me, but the strange acoustics, and the constant melody of the winds stopped me from guessing their direction.

Doris and Ace joined me at the foot of the ladder. We

set off, following the corridor.

The lights blinked off, dropping us into sudden darkness.

Something moved right beside me.

I pressed my ear to the wall, and heard footfalls again. Shoes on stone, the pitch of the notes changing as they descended stairs.

Doris lit a match, and the shadows drew back a little. A little further ahead, the corridor ended at a junction. The right hand branch would, I considered, lead us around the pyramid room and dining room to the kitchen. The left hand branch took us to the sound of footsteps.

The match was burning close to Doris's fingertips.

I turned left, and the corridor instantly doubled back on itself. One side of the corridor was the wooden panelling, the other was the rotting, crumbling bricks of the ruins. Overhead was a loom of thick cables.

There was a fuse box, the fuses scattered on the floor.

I ran over, and shoved the fuses back in.

The lights flickered to life. There were two doorways in the brick wall. We tried the closest. It opened out into the ruins, to a section of the manor where one of the walls had collapsed, a corner of the wing reduced to rubble. A section of fallen wall had become a platform on which a pair of diesel generators thrummed away.

I tried the other door.

It opened onto spiral stairs down into the vaults. The smell of smoke wafted upwards, and stung our eyes. I braced myself, and dropped a flash bomb my cuff down to my fingers. I stepped carefully down, pressing against the wall. Doris was right behind me, but Ace remained at the top of the stairs.

The stairway opened to the vaults, and the sound of crashing waves echoed through the smoke.

"Professor!" Saxon's voice boomed through the vaults. "You shouldn't have come, Professor. Or you should have kept your mouth shut."

I peered around the edge of the stairs, and glimpsed his

shadow in an arch, some distance away. I ducked back to cover. "I meant what I said, Saxon. We can talk this through, and get off the island before anything else goes wrong."

I glimpsed a revolver, as two gunshots rang out and chipped the wall close to my head.

"Are you dead?" Saxon barked.

I didn't answer.

"Professor?" Saxon asked, in a sing song voice.

Doris crept a little way back up the stairs, and crouched, like a cobra coiling to strike.

I took a dentist's mirror from inside my jacket, and held it to see out into the vaults.

Saxon held his pistol ready and stepped out into the vaults, edging carefully towards the stairs. He was wearing dark fatigues, and a wool watch cap. He viewed the world down the iron sights of his revolver.

I held up my hand, and counted down on my fingers, as Saxon stepped closer, and closer…

Five, four, three…

I vanished my mirror.

Two. My heart was racing. Adrenaline burned away all my pain.

One.

I threw the flash bomb at his feet, in the same instant that Doris jumped forwards. Saxon cried out, shielding his eyes, as Doris crashed into him, kicking him off his feet. He tried to fight her back, but she got a hold on his wrist, and twisted it, until his bones snapped, and the gun fell away.

Her knee found his groin, and he doubled over with a strangled cry. He fell to the floor, and rolled over, gawping in silent pain, like a fish drowning in air.

I scooped up the gun, and pointed it at Saxon.

"Ace!" I shouted. "Go and fetch the others. Saxon will tell us where his boat is, now."

"And the money?" Ace asked.

"Yes!" Saxon gasped.

Doris grinned.

*

We sat outside, on the grassy slopes around the ruins, and watched the police boats coming around the coast, and veering away from Whitt and towards the islands. Jack sat on a boulder, with Saxon, the service revolver held level and steady at the brooding magician. Saxon's broken whist was tethered over his heart, by an improvised sling.

Seven and Doris were sat on the blanket they found in the kitchen, sipping fresh coffee and making small talk.

"I'm going to the cave," I told them. "To put the lights on."

Doris set her coffee aside, and hurried after me.

"Hey," she said.

I turned, and faced her, cupping her cheek. "Hello."

Doris reached up, and held my hand to her. "You are shaking."

I nodded. "I never killed somebody before. I'm not… used to having brawls."

Doris smiled. "Me neither. Needs must!"

"You seemed rather… practised at it."

She laughed. "I have had to fend for myself before, and…" She looked at me. "I wasn't going to stand by and see you shot."

"Thank you."

She nodded. "And thank you." Her smile grew a little more confident. "So, did I need to look for a room for the next week or so? Or… Did you want to swap and let me take the sofa?"

"Let's see if I'm held on remand or not."

Doris closed her eyes, and stepped forwards to hug me. "I'm not losing you. Whatever happens." She took my hand. "Lets go and put those lights on."

Harry and Ace had taken the speedboat to the mainland, to summon a rescue. They had chosen not to head to Whitt, being unsure who to trust, and aim for a bigger town, with a police station.

A blur of minutes later, I was making off the police boats at the wharf in the cave. Uniformed officers swarmed onto the island.

PART FOUR

PUZZLES

Seventeen

I slept little in the months that followed. Butler's ghost was never quite allowed to rest in peace, and kept being shaken from his grave to haunt me, as I relived his death over and again.

First in the many hours of police interviews that followed our return to the mainland. Then at the coroner's court proceedings, and then for Saxon's long and arduous trial.

I gave evidence as best and honestly as I could, recounting my part, with the dreadful moments, and the crack of a skull on marine wood, echoing forever in the back of my mind, and the memories waiting to haunt me every night.

More often than not, either I, or Doris, were kept away by our troubles, and we lay together, talking softly in the darkness, or playing at the tricks I was trying to teach her. We kissed often, and whispered 'love you' whenever we could, while the world felt such a fragile place.

Through it all, the press was rabid with speculation and theories.

Saxon basked in it, he gloried in it, but I did not. It turned my stomach, and made the weight of the days harder to take.

Shortly before the trial, Inspector Plummer came to find me in the lockup. We went to the pub to talk.

"Tell me again," he said, evenly, "about the cheque Mandrake Saxon wrote you?"

I explained about the tricks I sold. He watched me carefully as I spoke.

"You know," he said, easing back in his chair, "that in my line of work we get a feeling for the truth. We aren't always perfect, and I wouldn't want to pretend I can always spot a lie… But I get a good feeling for when somebody is speaking the painful truth. It hurts the soul in a way that lies can't. You hate knowing where that money came from, don't you?"

"I keep thinking back to it all," I said, softly, "over and over, in an endless loop, trying to find whatever it is I should have seen before, to change what happened. I was in his workshop, I spoke to him, I… should have seen something, anything, in the threat, or the beating, or the letter, to put all of this together. I keep trying to find a way I could have stopped the deaths, or the heartache, or the fear…"

Plummer shook his head. "I had somebody try to tell me, and I thought he was lost in one of his usual fairy tales. I have to live with that."

I looked at my hands. "Maybe there wasn't a way, but there should have been, and…" I sighed. "I don't know. It just always feels like there is something I missed."

Plummer cleared his throat. "The question I wanted to ask is… delicate. I thought it was better asked off the record."

"Go on."

He lowered his voice. "Do you truly not know where Daniel Rochelle is?"

I shook my head. "No."

"If you are saying that to protect him from charges you feel would be..." The Inspector hesitated and chose his words carefully. "Too close to the values we fought against in the war..."

"No. Sir, I do not know where he is. If Harry knows, she did not tell me."

"Ah." He sipped his beer. "Another painful truth. You sympathise with him, and you wish you could protect him, but you can not." He tapped a pipe out, and refreshed the tobacco. "Let me assure you, that should he reach out to you, then my interest in him is purely in seeing the truer evil caged. His evidence could point to how, and when, Saxon or his agent got those photographs. It would make my case against Saxon stronger, and might offer us more of his network."

"I understand," I promised.

*

The trial was a living Hell for Harry, as it was for Jack,

Ace and Seven. The barristers were merciless and dogged in their pursuit of every possible point they could score, as they tried to turn the favour of the jury against the victims. They tried to drag us all over the coals, digging out whatever details of the guilty secrets they could.

Through it all, even as his guilt seemed assured, Saxon sat there, watching it all with a superior smile. He played to the audience, with a twinkle in his eye and a little joke, where the judge would rather have had a straight answer. When charged with being in contempt of court, he happily assured the judge he held everything of the trial in contempt.

After long weeks, and each of us being ground down under the millstone, the verdict was returned, and sentence was passed.

Saxon was still smiling.

*

A few weeks after the trial, Doris accepted an invitation for both of us to have a meal with Harry. It was at a fashionably expensive venue, in central London. As we rode the tube across the city, Doris snuggled against me, full of giggly, fluttery energy.

"So…" She smiled at me. "Who do you think he is?"

"The new man?" I shrugged. "I don't know. Somebody… nice."

"Nice?" Doris sighed. "No. I think he will have to be… dashing. And kind. And…"

"All the things I'm not?" I asked.

"Rich and good in bed?" Doris asked, with a giggle.

"Ouch!" I said.

She flashed me a triumphant smile in the moment before we kissed.

One of the other passengers chuckled behind their newspaper. "Both are accurate, but hardly her reasons." Jack lowered his broadsheet, and grinned at us both. He was dressed in the kind of suit that was razor sharp smart, masquerading as casual. "I hoped they were just… the garnish on my better qualities."

"Jack?" Doris asked with a laugh.

"Derby," he corrected her. "Sorry. Even in the trial, I kept notes. Who was who." He chuckled, and looked at me. "I thought I was so clever, having 'deduced' you were Harry's brother, even before Sir Perry told us. Except… you aren't."

"Sorry," I said.

Doris nudged me. "Everybody thought that?"

Derby nodded a little. "We rather did, I'm afraid. Ah. Do you think we should get off together, or should we just take it on the chin that I ruined Harry's surprise?"

"Together," Doris said. "We'll have a unified front."

I nodded. Something I couldn't put my finger on was spinning out of control at the back of my head. "So did Saxon, until he saw me."

Doris glanced at me. "Good. We made his life a little more difficult."

Thoughts began to take shape in my head, that were an unpleasant shape. They didn't make sense. Unless… Oh dear.

Oh no.

I tried to tell myself I was wrong.

I tried to find a reason I was wrong, but couldn't. And so my world fell apart around me.

"Simon?" Doris asked, softly.

I put my head in my hands.

"Simon?" Doris asked, suddenly concerned. "Are you okay?"

"I'm sorry," I said, with a croak, my throat dry and rasping, as my heart ground into a higher gear. "I might be about to completely ruin everybody's evening."

"Why?" Derby asked.

"Because… I need to ask Harry for a favour." I looked at Doris. "I know where her brother is."

NINETEEN

Harry let us in Rochelle's through the back. We hustled into the freight elevator, and Harry pulled on the lever.

I gave her a sorry smile. "Bert will know you touched that."

Harry shuddered. "I know. He always did when I was a kid."

Doris and Derby shared confused looks.

"It's a shop thing," Harry said.

"Ah." Derby (who I still wanted to call Jack) said. "I see."

Harry slowed us to a stop. "Tenth floor. Offices, utilities and the telephone exchange." She pulled open the doors. "What exactly are you looking for?"

I stepped out onto the floor, and followed the corridor around the offices and other rooms, tracing the route of the service corridor beneath. I opened a couple of doors and looked inside. Two offices, with a considerable walk between their doors, but both too modest in proportions to use the whole of the walk between them.

I inspected the blank corridor wall. "No flies?"

"We finally got rid of them," Harry said. "It took forever, but we found a contractor that could kill them off for good."

I ducked back into the nearest of the two offices, and dragged out a chair. I set it beneath the hatch in the ceiling. "This is a service space," I said. "Water pipes, air vents, and cables run behind there. I thought this would be a crawl space, but from the size, I think it's one of the old water tanks, from the original heating. It's all been renewed since, but..." I lifted the hatch open, and pulled down the short ladder. "Shall I take a look?"

Harry smiled. "And you think that is where my brother is hiding? Simon, I trusted you over this, but right now¬"

"Harry," I said, firmly, "please stop pretending not to know your brother is dead."

She froze and went white. Her eyes darted around. "What?" She asked.

"What?" Doris demanded.

I pointed at the wall. "He was dead long ago. Before the letter. Before you came for me for help. Before you sent Thorn to beat me up."

Harry went white. She shook her head. "How dare you? That is a disgusting thing to suggest!"

"She's right," Derby said. "Sorry, but I think this has all got to you."

"Harry," Doris said, calmly, softly, and gently, "just tell me you know nothing of this."

Harry opened her mouth and shook her head. Tears rolled down her cheeks.

"Harry," Doris said. "Please!"

Harry turned slowly, and stared up at me, tears filling her eyes. "How did you know?"

I climbed the ladder, and peeked through the false ceiling to the ancient water tank set amongst the web of air ducts, heating pipes, and asbestos clad pipes. There were countless dead flies around the tank. "I realised I was meant to die on the island. That raised the question of why." I pulled on a lever. It groaned. "Am I right?"

"Don't!" Harry pleaded. "Please."

I hesitated. "Why?"

Harry sobbed. "Because he is in there, with his service pistol. It… can't be mistaken for suicide. He was shot six times, in the back of his head. Please don't. The smell… I hate the smell."

I let go of the hatch on the tank, and slithered back down onto the ladder.

Doris and Derby were holding Harry in very hard stares.

Doris spoke first. "He was meant to die?"

Harry nodded. "Butler was meant to shoot him."

Doris looked up at me. "And when did you know that?"

"On the tube," I said. "It all kind of… dropped into place. Why Butler chose me, to drag out of the crowd and shoot me. Why did he think I had killed Thorn?"

"Because," Derby muttered, "he was under orders."

I stared into Harry's eyes. They were cold, dark, and lifeless, as jet. "He was under orders to kill me, and presumably, when Doris joined our endeavour, her as well. Because Doris wasn't meant to be there when the plan was made. Because she needed everybody to see Danny being shot, and killed, by a shotgun blast that would ruin his face."

Doris flinched as realisation hit her. "So she could never possibly have killed him… weeks before and hundreds of miles away!"

Harry shook her head. "To save the shop! To save everything!"

"If Danny was murdered by somebody else," I said, "she would have inherited his shares and influence in the store. She could undo all his changes."

Harry nodded. "We argued. He made me so mad. I… I…" She sighed. "What else?"

"You took the photos of Danny," I said. "You offered

them to Saxon, if he helped you with the problem at hand. If he let you clear up your problem, you could tell him all the gay men Danny knew, and he would have many, many, new targets.”

“But,” Doris said, “we saw her buying…” She blinked. “No. We saw a folder. It could have had anything in, to stuff it out. We just assumed it was the photographs.”

“And while we waited outside?” I asked. “She could have gone to the docks, and killed Thorn.”

“No!” Harry shook her head. “That was Saxon. He… tried to help me. To cover our tracks. He had Butler ordered to¬”

Doris shouted over her: “But you knew?”

Harry nodded.

Derby closed his eyes. “My god. That monster was meant to escape. You fed him more targets? He could… his organisation may still be at work!”

Harry shrugged. “I needed a deal with a devil.” She looked at me. “It was nothing personal.”

Doris chewed her lip. "What happens now."

"Now…" Harry reached into her purse for a sleek, waspish automatic pistol. She pointed it at Doris. "I have this plan. You see, Saxon still holds my part in the scheme over me. He knows of the body, and… the only reason I can see for him not revealing it at trial, is because he intends to use that knowledge, sooner, or later. I need to change the story. What if there was a gas explosion, and a fire, caused by obvious sabotage? And he was found nearby? It would be logical to believe he was murdered confronting the arsonist, one of Saxon's agents, that… you all died, when clever old Simon somehow discovered the plan and… you all helped him… no… *we* helped him, and almost stopped him, but they had guns… And the gas pipe runs, right there, and…"

"And after," I said, my voice cold, "you will use the insurance to rebuild the store in the model you wanted. A new store with the old values."

Doris stared at the gun. "Harry, please. You don't want to do this."

"No." Harry took the slack from the trigger. "But I have to, or... I have to survive. You can see that? Can't you?"

I braced myself on the ladder. "Harry, point the gun at me."

She glanced up at me. "I'm not stupid, she is the one who¬"

I kicked Harry's wrist away. The gun swung away from the others. Doris stepped forwards, putting all her weight, all her power, all her speed behind a brutal uppercut. It sent Harry flying backwards, to land in a heap.

The gun slid across the floor. Derby stepped on it. He sighed and crouched down, to look at Harry, with despair in his eyes. "Harry... have you learned nothing? There is only one way to be free of Saxon's leverage."

Harry groaned in dismay.

TWENTY

Doris was a dab hand at welding. She was hiding behind a mask, helping me put together a frame for my latest prototype. She was grubby, sweaty, and smiling in a way that gave my butterflies fluttery-shivers. She was beautiful.

She stepped back, and lifted her goggles. She gave me one of those looks. "What?"

I flushed. "Nothing, I just…"

She chuckled, and chewed her lip. "I know you do."

There was a knock on my door, as Tony popped his head in. "Hello?"

"Tony!" I walked over. "Doris, this is my agent, Tony. Tony, this is my…"

"Beautiful assistant?" Tony asked, with a wink.

"Hardly!" Doris glanced at me. "If you ever get me on stage, it will be the Professors, plural."

Tony chuckled. "Hey… they might like that…"

"Who?" I enquired.

Tony tugged on his braces. "Well, it turns out that Mandrake Saxon is unable to meet his obligations, and there are some bookings open. Like the summer long engagement headlining the Beachside Variety Bill, in the Wintergarden Theatre."

My shoulder's slouched.

Doris's straightened. "Oh? And you just happened to mention that you had the notorious witness from that court case on your books?"

Tony mimed pain in his heart. "No! I told them I had a magician on my books who sold Saxon some of his more impressive tricks. They are interested. They want you to audition for them." He cocked his head at the framework. "This looks… interesting. Is it something that will impress them?"

"It impresses me," Doris said, "and I know how it is going to work."

Tony rubbed his hands. "What's it going to do?"

"It turns somebody into butterflies," Doris said.

"And back again," I promised.

"Maybe…" Doris narrowed her eyes.

Tony laughed. "Is she any good?"

Doris flicked her wrist. There was a pop of springs, and a cigarette flew out of her sleeve, and span in the air. She caught the filter between her teeth, and conjured a matchstick with a click of her fingers, striking the head with her thumb, and lighting the cigarette in a single, fluid, motion. "What do you think?"

Tony's eyes lit up with the prospect of another paying client, at his usual rate. "I think you two are going to spend the summer doing the kind of work that doesn't make you sleep in a bloody shed."

Doris grabbed my hand. "We want the audition."

I smiled. "We do."

"Professors!" Doris whispered. "Plural." She blew out some smoke. "How long a routine do we need?"

*

We stood across the road, and watched the signs being changed on the front of Rochelle's. It wasn't just the font being changed. The decorators had stripped away the conservative window displays, and replaced them with something a little more daring, and atomic aged, looking towards the future.

Doris leant her head on my shoulder. "Do you think this counts as an ending, or a new beginning?"

"That," I said, "depends on if Bert is still working the freight elevator."

Doris squeezed my hand. "I choose to make it the beginning of something…."

"Something better?" I asked.

She laughed, and stepped around me, moving in for a kiss. "The very best."

The kiss was a fleeting promise of more. She stepped away, her fingers still curled about mine. I followed her, as she vanished into the crowd.

www.ingramcontent.com/pod-product-compliance
Lightning Source LLC
Chambersburg PA
CBHW071613150726
48000CB00004B/1711